# FLOWER KING

A MODERN SHAKESPEARE HANAHAKI TALE

Keep an eye out for this next adventure

THE
*Basement*
WIZARD

# FLOWER KING

Riley Tyler

FLOWER KING: A BENVOLIO X MERCUTIO
HANAHAKI TALE

Published by Booktastic
ISBN Paperback 979 8 89965 204 2
ISBN (Hardcover) 978 94 6266 769 3
First Edition, Limited

Front cover image by Peony
Vector art: Blossom: ThaiLy on Pixabay
**www.RileyTyler.com**

Key Words
Romance, Young Adult, Drama & Angst, Mutual
Pining, Hanahaki Disease, Man x Man, Benvolio
Montague, Mercutio Escalus

This is a work of fiction loosely based on
Shakespeare's 'Romeo and Juliet'. Any names or
characters, businesses or places, events or incidents
different from those in Shakespeare's original play
are fictitious. Any resemblance to actual persons,
living or dead, or actual events is purely coincidental.

Dedicated to

# The Queer Boekenkast

*Thomas & Valentijn*

*Prologue* ........................................ 9

*Chapter One* ...................................14

*Chapter Two* ..................................44

*Chapter Three* ...............................67

*Chapter Four* .................................84

*Chapter Five* ..................................96

*Chapter Six* ...................................110

*Chapter Seven* ..............................126

*Chapter Eight* ...............................146

*Chapter Nine* ................................164

*Chapter Ten* ..................................170

*Chapter Eleven* .............................187

*Chapter Twelve* .............................200

*Chapter Thirteen* ..........................219

*Chapter Fourteen* .........................229

*Chapter Fifteen* .............................243

*Chapter Sixteen* ............................258

*Chapter Seventeen* .......................271

*Chapter Eighteen* .........................290

Acknowledgments .........................309

# *Prologue*

It started slowly, with just one petal. Why I didn't dare to tell anyone about it, I don't know. I was too caught up in whatever I had just witnessed to worry about it. And trust me, what I had seen had shaken me to the core. As time passed, more petals came, but I was too busy keeping an eye on Romeo. As always, he was on the road to getting his fancy self into trouble. But that's my cousin for you.

Welcome to my life. My name is Benvolio Montague. Contrary to what many people believe about me, I am not a minor character leeching on the story threads of others like a desperate, glittering vampire. Although it sometimes feels as if I am hidden in the shadows, when I remember how long I have been chasing Romeo to keep him from doing something foolish. I don't always succeed, though.

Many people in Verona know me because of Romeo. He is my cousin, and we're about the same age, so I am often seen by his side. I suppose that is why people tend to refer to me as 'Lord Montague's nephew' or 'Romeo's cousin' rather than just *Benvolio Montague*.

I suppose I cannot blame them. Lord Montague, Romeo's father and my uncle, is quite the celebrity in Verona. He owns a prosperous business emporium, which adds to his fame. Everyone knows him, and thus, everyone knows Romeo. In contrast, my parents work ordinary jobs and lead simple lives far from the spotlight.

I am aware that some people think I am an orphan. It's probably because of the large number of orphaned Capulets roaming the city. I am thinking of Tybalt in particular. Like me, he is the nephew of a famous businessman. But unlike me, he has been taken in by his uncle. So, I do understand why people assume my uncle took me in as well. However, I have my own apartment, and my parents are both alive and healthy, thank you very much.

I wish I could say as much about myself. Alive. *Barely*. Healthy. *I'll get to that*.

When we wander the streets, there aren't just the two of us. We are with three. Romeo's best friend is always there with us.

Mercutio.

*My best friend*.

When I look at him parading through the alleyways of Verona, I feel my heart skip a beat. Mercutio isn't the most logical friend for me. He's outgoing and wild. His bravery often surpasses his wit. While I am tender of nature, more secluded. I like to keep to myself, and if it hadn't been for Romeo, I would have happily

[10]

spent my days staring out of the window, practicing my hand at calligraphy, or playing unnecessarily elaborate games that use a tremendous amount of fantasy. Because I am a dreamer, in a way. And it just so happens to be that Mercutio, despite the facade, is a dreamer just the same.

Let me spare him another thought before I tell you exactly how I am feeling today, because Mercutio's description is far from done yet.

How did we become friends when he is so lively and so spirited? I can hear you ask. It's because he sought out Romeo when we were younger. The two are always searching for boundaries and how to cross them. Without a guiding hand, they'd always be in trouble. That is where I come in. Let that guiding hand be me.

Mercutio is the nephew of Verona's 'Prince'. He is not a real prince, by the way. That is just his first name. And rather fanciful for one of Italy's most influential politicians. So, needless to say, Mercutio comes from a ridiculously wealthy family and has money aplenty. *Once he reaches the age of thirty, that is.*

It's as simple as that, and it has managed to be a sore spot for him ever since he found out about it. That doesn't mean he is penniless. He still receives an abundant amount of pocket money and spends most of it on ridiculous blue and purple denim jackets and on the coloring of his hair. It's fuchsia at the moment. He had to explain that to me over and over because I kept calling his hair pink.

As you might have guessed, he isn't your typical macho man, either. He knows all about fashion, actors, and models, keeps his own ridiculous *Tumblr* account, and has an *Instagram* he spams full of selfies. He actually has a lot of followers online, as well. It's ridiculous.

His free time is spent browsing photos of—as he calls it—*pussies*, which are actual cat photos that sometimes make me cringe. I am certain he suffers from Toxoplasmosis. Which reminds me, he teasingly calls Tybalt his famous 'Prince of Cats'. I am not quite certain what to make of it.

My feelings for him are, well, complicated. Trust me, I have tried on several occasions to probe his emotional defense and find out who or what he fancies in others. I tried to burst through his carefully crafted shield of the happy-go-lucky boy he pretends to be, never worried or sad, and always with a proper joke on the tip of his tongue.

*How I wish he would tell me something. How to stand a chance. Or if I ever could.*

For a long time, Mercutio sided with the Capulets. They own a rival company to the Montagues, so there's been bad blood between

[12]

the two families for quite a while. This ongoing 'feud' matters because it means Capulets and Montagues usually either steer clear of each other, or end up in fights.

Mercutio's best Capulet friend is Rosaline. We all knew that he initially got closer to her because Romeo had a crush on her and didn't know how to approach her. So, Mercutio took the lead and showed him the ropes. He became friends with her in record time. But then she thought he was trying to make advances on her and admitted she was asexual. Mercutio stuck to the same label for a few months afterward, claiming to be asexual as well when he clearly couldn't take his eyes off men and women alike. I teased him about it, but he claimed he was just admiring their sense of fashion. *As if.*

But as it turned out, Mercutio was not asexual.

And that was when the first petal got stuck down my throat, making me grab my neck in an attempt not to choke. I had never before felt as suffocated as this, not even in a hands-on fight.

It was when I spotted Mercutio in the arms of another.

[13]

# *One*

The night was young, or so Romeo kept reminding me. I was tired, but I agreed to hang out with him anyway. God knew how much trouble he would get himself into if it weren't for me to keep him out of it.

"Let me call Rosaline," I said, reaching for my phone, but Romeo placed his hand on top of mine and smiled cheekily.

"No need, I've already done that." I looked up at him quizzically. His dazzling smile did nothing to ease my nerves. Romeo's dark eyes twinkled. His hair, reminiscent of my own, pale and coiffed to the front, made him stand out among the dirty gray tiles of the street and the walls.

We stood in front of the small alley next to the movie theater. A crowd of youngsters had gathered in front of the movie theater's doors, pushing and pulling and being boisterous for the whole city to hear. This new movie that would be shown for the first time in Verona was said to be the next giant blockbuster. By the looks of the many attendees, it was indeed going to be the talk of the town. The fact that the movie was R-rated and starred a few sexy young actresses and a lot of violence might have something to do with it. I wasn't looking forward to seeing it, but since Romeo had taken it upon himself to buy us tickets, what choice was I left with?

"You're still trying?" I asked, stupefied. "Man, you've got to let go. Rosaline isn't into your type. She isn't into anyone who wants to get their hands on her."

Instead of looking stumped, Romeo smiled at me as if my words hadn't affected him in the slightest. "I asked her to bring Livia."

That shut me up. So Rosaline's younger sister had been invited too? I wasn't sure why Romeo kept trying to bring me and Livia together all the time. Was it because we had become good friends?

*Oh yes,* while the two buffoons I called my friends struggled to get themselves a date, I had grown closer to both Rosaline and Livia. I knew Romeo wondered how I had achieved this. I suppose by just being normal around them and showing genuine interest. *If only my cousin would watch and learn.*

Livia was two years younger than Rosaline and loved to draw. In my opinion, she was starting to become quite an artist. Naturally, Mercutio tried to abuse the girl's talents by trying to trick her into drawing portraits of him that he could later post to his socials. *So vain.* She sometimes obliged him. But more often than not, she would draw pictures of the sea instead. She loved nature and drawing landscapes. Although impeccable in every genre, her style was often used to depict her surroundings rather than the people she met.

So the Capulet sisters were considered our friends, and if it hadn't been for the entire Montague-Capulet thing, we could have met out in the open rather than try and do these things secretly. I admit it is all a rather odd circumstance. Capulets and Montagues don't usually go together that well. Yet Rosaline and Livia seemed more approachable. Perhaps because they weren't locked away from the Montague part of the city like most of the Capulet girls. They attended a public school, didn't react to Montagues' shouts in the streets, and seemed unaffected by the feud that raged between the two families in general. *They almost seemed normal.*

Snapping back to the here and now, I looked up at Romeo's incriminating smile and wanted to whack him on the head. I knew what he must be thinking. By bringing Livia along, she could keep me distracted, giving him the chance to talk and try and seduce Rosaline. He wanted a romance so badly that he had become blind to all forms of reason. No matter how often I had warned him that Rosaline wasn't interested, he kept believing that he could change her mind. I could only pray that Mercutio wouldn't be too busy with his phone and taking selfies so that he could interfere on my behalf.

*Come to think of it*, "Where's Mercutio? Won't he be joining us?" An evening spent without my fuchsia-headed friend was time well wasted. I looked at Romeo and let out a sigh. My cousin's eyes slid aside, turning to the concrete pavement beneath our feet as he lousily plucked at the fabric of his empty pockets. Out of the three of us, Romeo never had a dime on his person. I could explain this to you, but I already told you that he had bought tickets for all of us. If you've been counting correctly, you'll have noticed that there are no longer two or three entrance tickets to a movie's premiere… but five.

"He'll be on his way," Romeo said, his words like a salve, and I sighed in relief. Thank goodness God invented Mercutio. Now, I wouldn't have to take care of Romeo on my own. Rosaline would need all the protection she could get, and besides, if I wanted to spend some of our time tonight talking and laughing with Livia, I really needed Mercutio's extra pair of hands to keep Romeo restrained in his cinematic seat.

"Hellokidoki," *speak of the devil*. I saw Romeo look up almost synchronically with me. Our eyes met for a brief moment before they slid to the figure who had joined us. Mercutio was looking as fine as always. His lithe body was

[17]

covered in blue silk, and he carried with him a black leather jacket with spikes. Out of the three of us, Mercutio was the one who made a point of wearing a jacket with the word 'Montague' on the back, complete with shiny diamonds and all. The word had been glued on this particular jacket by hand. I appreciated his creative skills, but still, I wondered why he wrote our name on all of his jackets. It must be a feud thing, to show which side he was on. He wasn't a Montague himself.

From across the street, he winked at us, and I felt my knees go weak. There he was, standing at the corner of the alleyway and the street, leaning backward against a wall, his jacket draped casually over one shoulder. With two fingers, he held the leather in its place.

The sight of him made my mouth turn dry, and with a quick clearing of my throat, I started to walk toward him. His grin expanded when I approached.

"And a good day to you, too, fine gentleman," I said before I bowed mockingly. He returned the gesture. It was our little greeting, mostly because we never got Romeo to stoop as low as to join us whenever we greeted each other this way. *The spoilsport.* "How nice of you to have decided to join us."

"Aren't the chicks here yet?" Mercutio asked, decidedly ignoring my teasing and

[18]

quirking a brow at Romeo instead.

There was something hidden in the way Mercutio's eyes lay upon Romeo. The glint in his beautiful, dark orbs was almost akin to disapproval. But because of what? Because Romeo was still trying to seduce Rosaline?

I studied him; his lips pressed into a thin-lipped pout, the crease of his brow, and the little line between his eyes that shaped whenever he was frowning heavily. It was cute, *almost*.

"They should be here any minute," Romeo said, a charming smile plastered across his face like always. "Here, did you bring any money? I'm afraid I spent all of mine ordering the tickets, and I've got nothing left to pay for the popcorn to have you guys fed."

Mercutio playfully quirked a brow. His arms were folded in front of his chest now, jacket crumpled between his elbow and hand. "You realize I'm more a rich-flavor kind of kid?"

"Come on, bro," Romeo instantly retorted. He had stepped closer and now stood in front of Mercutio, facing him, and hunched slightly forward so that they were about the same size. Their eyes were at the same level, caught in a stare. "Whenever we buy popcorn, you eat half of mine. Just get your own bag and pay for your own chocolate addiction, and we call it a draw."

Out of all of us, Mercutio definitely ate

[19]

the most despite being the thinnest. So, apart from suffering from Toxoplasmosis, I also highly suspected him of housing a tapeworm somewhere in there. *It's unfair for anyone to be this lean and slender if all they did was eat all day.*

Then again, Mercutio was also the most active and probably needed all of it to keep his energy levels up. He was a fanatic when it came to parkour, running across buildings like he had wings. *It was truly a sight to behold.* He was also usually very chipper, not to mention hyper 24/7. I often wished I could own even a modicum of his energy.

I stood next to my cousin in front of Mercutio. "Romeo's right," I said, quickly counting inside my head. I still had some coins in my pocket that I had wanted to save to buy Livia a present. Not for her birthday, but just because it seemed nice. I had seen some appealing digital drawing pens shaped like quills in the store window earlier that day. They were quirky and exclusive, and I figured that if I could save for another week, I might be able to buy one for her.

"Besides," I continued, "he's already benevolently gifted us the tickets, so I suppose if one of us bought the food, that would only be fair."

But it seemed my words were met by deaf ears. Mercutio rolled his eyes to the sky and let out an exaggerated sigh.

"Fair? Fair, dear Ben?" His finger tapped against his elbow rapidly while he looked away and shook his head. "The only thing fair here is your hair," he hesitated and turned toward Romeo. "And yours," he added whilst chewing his lower lip. "So please don't make me laugh, or the clock will strike twelve, and my face will forever look this way." As if to add strength to his words, he twisted his lips and rolled his eyes till they were crossed, the gaze ridiculously enough to make Romeo next to me chuckle.

I grinned at Mercutio's antics, unable to suppress a smile of my own. He was so theatrically gifted that I always wondered why he had never considered joining an acting troupe. *He'd be amazing on stage.* "Better be frozen in a smile than in a chagrined grimace," I replied. But as soon as I said it, I regretted it.

Mercutio's eyes twinkled when he looked at me. Then, without a warning, he burst through the wall Romeo and I had created by standing in front of him. He was by now singing at the top of his lungs, a very famous tune that was bound to have many heads turned our way. *What had I done?*

"Let it go, let it go—"

"Did you say *Frozen*?" Romeo asked me, and I gulped, knowing exactly that Mercutio's off-key singing had been *my fault.* I glanced at

[21]

him from over my shoulder. *Yep, the people in line for the movie theater were watching us.* I could only hope the girls would be here soon so we could head inside, or that some kind of miracle would happen to shut our friend up.

"I'm sorry, okay," I stuttered to Romeo, who looked at me with compassion. "Just let me make up for it. How about I go pay for all the snacks, and we'll not argue about it any longer?" I glanced nervously at Mercutio, who, although he gave me a sidelong glance, kept to his song. Clearly, he wasn't in the mood to buy the treats for us. *While he has the most money of us all,* I thought sourly.

Romeo handed me my ticket without delay, but there was a look of sympathy on his face. *Good.* At least part of him was aware that his brilliant setup was going to cost *me* a lot of money. Perhaps he would be thinking twice before spending all his dough on silly movie tickets next time.

"Popcorn for all of us, salty for Livia and for me, sweet for the others," Romeo instructed me as I tucked the ticket in my breast pocket. I shrugged, nothing unexpected in his request there.

"Anything else?" I looked up at him. "Drinks?"

Romeo seemed to hesitate, a pensive expression in his eyes, but I was too impatient to leave my singing friend to stick around until he had finally thought of an answer. "Never mind, I'll see what I can carry."

Romeo nodded. "Meet us in the lobby. We'll head inside as soon as the girls arrive. It's not as warm as it used to be."

I could see how Romeo wrapped his arms around him and suppressed a shiver. His thin shirt clung tightly to his body, accentuating his abs.

"Well, it's the evening screening," I said while I stifled a laugh. "Perhaps you should have put on something warmer. Why didn't you bring your jacket?"

Romeo laughed softly and imitated the shrug I had done earlier. *I knew exactly why he hadn't. The show-off.* Anyone with brains could tell that leaving his coat at home was stupid. An action in vain, as Rosaline had no interest in him or his abs. Plus, he now missed the chance of pulling the ultimate gentleman move and offering her his coat once the temperatures started to drop.

With a smile on my face, I turned away from him and made my way to the entrance of the towering building. Red swirly neon lights formed the name of the movie theater on top of the edge of the roof. I had to apologize for passing through the lines that had formed in front. Eager youngsters stood waiting to buy

[23]

their tickets, hoping they wouldn't run out before their turn was due. I realized how lucky we were that Romeo had gotten ours in advance. *Even if it was a waste of money, technically. Speaking of which...*

My hand dug deep inside my pocket. *I was going to lose it*, my own hard-earned money. I didn't work in a store selling shoes to spend my money on this. *Candy.* To see a movie I really wasn't interested in.

I passed the doors in haste, wanting to get away from Mercutio's public display as fast as possible. One last glance over my shoulder, and I could see him circling the lamppost. *Oh my God.* One slender hand was curled tightly around the cold metal of the post. A nicely shaped leg wrapped around it, joining the hand in its caressing of the pole. My cheeks colored in embarrassment. Deep inside, I knew that I actually enjoyed his little show. *Who knew Mercutio was such a nimble pole dancer?*

I quickened my pace, eager to get the image from my mind. But once I was inside, the urge to escape from the embarrassing scene had vanished. I trudged to the counter selling food and drinks.

Once in front of it, it took me a moment to realize what I was looking at. Mercutio just does that to you, at least to me. My mind sometimes has to reset after seeing him pull one

[24]

of his jokes.

In front of me, I saw bags filled with popcorn, different cases filled with colorful candies of all shapes and flavors, and on the counter was a mini fridge containing a small array of fizzy drinks. I looked up at the cashier but found her looking at me expectantly. I quickly swallowed.

My cheeks felt heated, probably flushing, as I felt embarrassed. I had been so caught up in my mind that I hadn't noticed I was at the front of the line. As is a habit, when you notice that it is your turn, I parted my lips to order. But my voice was drowned out by the sharp tones of another.

"Come to see the greatest movie of all time, I see?"

My head spun around instantly, knowing that voice and recognizing it with dread. My eyes clapped upon the red and purple dressed frame of no one other than Tybalt Capulet. A tall and slender young man with luscious black hair.

He was standing close to me, closer than I had initially assumed, and was surrounded by three girls. Each of them had their hair bleached, reminding me of my own light curls. Their red dresses were a bit too short, and their smirks too smug. Their hands were plastered on his shoulders as if they were girls he had picked up outside of some louche club late at night. And

[25]

that's a polite way of me trying to say how suspiciously unchaste and immoral the three looked, their hands roaming past Tybalt's body like he was some kind of god.

It was hard for me to imagine why anyone would like him, let alone adore him. Tybalt was the Capulets' most risky family member. Being Rosaline's and Livia's cousin, I had heard many a tale about him. Of course, I knew him from the street, where he was famous for shouting nasty things whenever our paths crossed. Tybalt was easily angered, short-tempered, and *always* armed. That last bit of knowledge made me take an involuntary step sideward, away from him and his supportive girls.

It'd be foolish to deny how much the man could intimidate me. He was slightly older and had the advantage in height and posture. That one-year difference felt like many, many more. Probably because he knew how to tower over us with his lean limbs.

You might think I would try and hide from him. That I would keep quiet and stand to the side like Romeo often does during these confrontations. But for some reason, Tybalt seemed to despise me the most and never gave me the chance to step away from a fight. But whenever we meet, he picks on me and makes sure I can't get away unseen. He even knows my name, which is rather unusual. He usually scolds the other Montagues and never bothers to remember them by name. Though here is one other name he remembers: *Mercutio*. It's the only other name he uses in our fights. If it isn't *'Benvolio, I'm gonna kill you,' it's usually, 'Come here, Mercutio, so I can plunge my knife in you.'*

Mercutio must probably be his favorite Montague supporter to insult. The two usually fight a lot, struggling with their lean limbs in some kind of sensual form of wrestling. But Mercutio always seems to know how to create a distance between them.

I am aware that Mercutio enjoys challenging the Capulet. He just loves to taunt him, loves the thrill it gives him whenever he gets away unscathed from another fight with the easy-to-rile-up Tybalt. Their insults are often funny to behold, and the youths of Verona love to watch them go at each other. We encourage them to fight. *It's just that entertaining.*

And every time Mercutio manages to get away from Tybalt, when he shouts filthy nicknames at him from a distance, Tybalt's rage only increases, and he screams so deliciously loud that I suspect everyone in Verona must be able to hear it.

I think that is the beauty of it all, and that is why Montagues and Capulets alike keep pushing the two together. They rage with such passion, and the least amount of broken bones from any of us.

Also, Mercutio always manages to slither away and leave Tybalt steaming with anger. What's not to love about such victories?

I trembled, an effect I wish I could conceal, but Tybalt had already noticed. His eyes narrowed and slid to my trembling hands. A small smile slipped onto his lips, tugging them into a nasty smirk.

"You don't have to answer. I can imagine how much it must surprise you that I would lower myself to talk to the likes of you."

Seething with anger, I gritted my teeth. My hands had curled into fists by my side, but I wouldn't dare to act. I told you that he gets violent easily, and I've been in too many fights with him to count. No one ever won a battle from Tybalt, except Mercutio. And Mercutio wasn't here to save me now.

"Na-ah, I wouldn't do that if I were you," Tybalt chided me, barely containing his glee. I forced my hands to relax enough to stretch my fingers.

"Now there's a good boy," Tybalt cooed. His voice was soft, but it had the sing-song tone one might use with a small child, which made it extremely patronizing to me. The girls at Tybalt's side laughed at my pitiful defense, which was me doing nothing but taking the

[28]

humiliation from the man in front of me.

"I suppose you came here with your little friends? One never catches a Montague dog on their own. Too frightened, right? Too eager to stick their tail between their legs and run for it. Go on, aren't you going to run?" He tilted his head and let out a short, boisterous laugh.

I had to bite my tongue. If Tybalt knew I was here with his cousins, what would he do? *Decapitate me? Hide my body in parts in the canals?* I dreaded to think about it.

"Oh, you scared puppy. Not even got the guts to bark," as he said it, he advanced on me, but he needn't have done that. I was already frozen with fright. He cocked his head, and his long dark tresses fell down his shoulder. "Not even going to try and woof us away?"

His eyes then slid from mine, breaking the silent, threatening stare between us and toward my mouth. His eyes narrowed once more, and I knew he had noticed the way I was gritting my teeth, trying to keep myself from commenting. "You're showing me such nice teeth, Benvolio, like the good little dog you are. That can only mean one thing. You want my help?"

I knew I would regret it, but I couldn't help but ask, "Help with what?"

"With your dentistry, of course. A hole between this one," he had the nerve to reach out,

[29]

his fingernail tapping against my canine, yet I couldn't bring myself to move or press my lips shut. He was too fast and too intimidating. Up this close, I could smell his Eau de Cologne. It was disgustingly heavy and musky, but despite its pungent intensity, I could still discern the underlying scent of sweat that was all Tybalt.

"And this one," he finished by tapping a tooth that was several away from the first, all located in the upper row, "would really improve your image. Give you a bit of a rough edge. What do you say, hm?"

The moment his finger left my teeth, I snapped my lips shut. Tybalt seemed displeased by my action and grunted. His eyes widened slightly before narrowing again, and his lips pressed into a thin, displeased line. But then he tilted his head to the side, the muscles in his neck cracking with a loud, sickening sound as he relieved the tension that must have been building up there. His nostrils flared as he took a deep breath, his expression calmer now. He must have expected me to close my lips at some point, right? If I had been braver, I could even have tried to bite his fingertip off. He must have expected something along those lines from me, right? Or had I become too predictable? Was he right when he said that I would never fight back?

Without a warning, he leaned into me.

His lips were close to my ear, so I could feel his hot breath upon my skin, sending goose bumps down my body. His whisper was too quiet for the girls by his side to hear, but loud enough to reach me. The message was loud and clear.

"You're too soft," he breathed. Then, before I could react, he leaned back and left me blinking, unable to think of any kind of comeback that would not result in giving him a reason to beat me up. I sincerely hoped that Romeo and Mercutio wouldn't come in while he was standing next to me. I dreaded to think of all that could happen if they saw how he was intimidating me. Or what would happen, indeed, if he saw that we were having a date with his cousins?

"You'd better not be taking the middle seats." Tybalt had finished ordering without me even realizing it. The girls each held a drink of their own. The one with the white and red dress carried a large bag of popcorn, presumably to share. "Or take the seat in front of us," Tybalt finished his threats. He tapped two fingers against his temple as a greeting before he turned around. The girls by his side followed him.

They were laughing at my expense.

"Hey, don't sweat it. If you take a seat in the back row, then you can attack him from the back." I looked up, speechless, into the face of the cashier. She smiled shyly and placed her

[31]

hands on the plastic surface of the counter in front of her. Her long, auburn hair swayed slightly as she moved one shoulder forward and looked at me through her long lashes. "I'm sorry, I meant to say, sitting behind them gives you some sort of an advantage, right?"

How much did she know about the clash between the Montagues and the Capulets? Was she a Montague supporter I had never heard of? Or could she become one?

I stammered, "right." It was kind of her to be concerned about me and my fate. It felt like I had found an ally I might need. *If Tybalt were to kill me today, then at least I had one witness I could count on.*

"Your order?" she asked, her voice gentle.

"Ah, right," I cleared my throat and dug my hand deep inside my pocket. "Popcorn," I swallowed and tried to clear my throat as I handed her the cash. The nerves were slowly starting to ebb away, but only because I'd thrown another look over my shoulder and saw no sign of the cursed Capulets.

"Two salty, three sweet, all small ones," I ordered. The cashier smiled at me while she set to work. She was joined by a male colleague who came out of a door behind her. He wore the same green apron and hat as she did, with a white blouse underneath, and showed a toothy smile upon seeing me.

"Hello, I see Juliet is already helping you?" he inquired curtly.

"Correct," I said, wondering how red my cheeks must be and how far that shade would stretch. I always turned red whenever I felt ashamed, shy, or intimidated. Whatever the reason, Mercutio always loved to remind me of how easily my face would flush. He called me 'the blushing bride' because of it. *God, if only he were here now to save me from placing a bumbling and clumsy order. What a fool I must look like after all that Tybalt has said to me.*

"Anything else with it, sir?" Juliet asked me kindly. She had put five small boxes of popcorn on the counter and inserted the prices into the cash register. It was one of those fancy old systems where you had to push buttons before the price popped up. Not one of those automatic scans that beeped all the products you sold.

"And these, please," I added, interrupting her before she could enter the 'pay' button and finish my order. I pointed at a candy bag with little chocolate-covered sweets. She looked up at me through the strands of her hair and smirked.

Seeing the coins left on the counter, I did a quick math and decided that, along with the food, I might as well buy everyone a drink, too.

[33]

Perhaps one of them would find it in their hearts to pay me back at a later date.

After ordering some lemon-lime sodas and colas — *why the hell did she give me that off-brand stuff? Romeo might drink that shit, but I quickly swapped to a citrus soda instead* — I tried to gather all the drinks, boxes, and bags into my arms, but I soon realized, dejectedly, that there was no way I could carry it all on my own into the lobby without growing an extra pair of arms.

Apparently, Juliet had seen my distress and quickly jumped to the rescue. She left her place behind the counter.

"Björn, would you take over the counter from me?" She called from over her shoulder, without so much as looking back at him. "I'm helping this customer."

When she reached my side, I stood with a brow raised in question. I didn't even need to voice my thoughts. *Such an unusual name.*

"He's an exchange student from Sweden," she said, almost as if she could read my mind, scooping the boxes and the bags into her arms. I have to say that she managed to carry a whole lot more in her arms than I could have managed. She had this very clever technique of stacking the boxes. She definitely had experience with this.

Balancing the bottles of drinks between my arms and chest, I marched forward. I felt the

[34]

disapproving glares from other moviegoers around me. The line outside was dwindling. More people entered the theater, looking hungry and thirsty. I could sense their frustration at seeing one of the two food sellers help me with my order. I hoped Romeo and the others were nearby to save me from this humiliation.

With a sigh of relief, I spotted my friends the moment we entered the lobby. Mercutio was seated on a beanbag, his long legs stretched in front of him, his leather boots resting on top of each other. He was staring up at Livia, who was telling him some kind of exciting tale.

Livia was wearing simple clothes. Her dark hair had been bleached, and she had added a few strands of red, the signature color of the Capulets. It was a rebellious act after her parents forbade her from dyeing her hair blue, the traditional color of my family. She had told me that she had bleached her hair to match mine instead, as a subtle tribute to the Montagues. I found it a sweet gesture.

Rosaline stood slightly behind them, her hair still dark, but she had joined her sister in getting the red highlights in. My eye instantly fell on the red jacket wrapped around her handbag. If she got cold, she wouldn't need anyone else's coat or jacket. My eyes slid to my cousin. Romeo had been suffering from the cold for nothing.

[35]

Upon seeing me, Rosaline tore herself away from the group and came rushing to my side. She looked horrified and instantly reached for the drinks I was balancing in front of me.

Romeo stood at the side of the group, leaning against a wall with his right foot propped against the plaster, chuckling as he scratched his head awkwardly. *At least he seemed to feel remorse for having sent me out on my own.*

"My God, did the fools make you get our food all by yourself?" Rosaline exclaimed, quickly taking some of the bottles from my arms and sharing them around.

"Erm, yes." I hesitated to look at them. "*And* I had to pay for it." *As if that extra bit of knowledge somehow couldn't be left out.* There was pity in Rosaline's eyes, and shame in Romeo's. Mercutio seemed unperturbed and ran a hand through his fuchsia-colored hair, flicking the longer strands to the side.

"And I see you brought us a new friend," Rosaline gestured toward Juliet, who had taken it upon herself to distribute the boxes, probably in a hurry to get back to the counter. I watched as the salty boxes landed in the hands of Mercutio and Romeo. *Well, at least one of them was delivered correctly.*

Romeo's eyes lit up and lingered on Juliet a little longer than was appropriate. *Oh no, not again…*

Mercutio, the only one not interested in Juliet's presence, started tasting his popcorn. With a foul expression, he stuck out his tongue and made gargling sounds. *Here it comes*, I thought with a smile while I watched him. *He is a 'sweet' kind of guy*.

"This is salty," Mercutio complained. Rosaline took the chocolates from Juliet and threw them into his lap, then took the box out of his hand. "*Baby*," she muttered while she swapped the popcorn with Livia's.

The latter was staring at me with little expression. It was odd to see Livia look at me that way. Usually, there was a hint of softness to her face, a ghost of a smile at the very least. But her face was bereft of emotion, and it sent a shiver down my spine.

*What had I done wrong?*

"Luckily, someone was chivalrous enough to help you," Rosaline added, bringing me out of my thoughts. She gave a pointed look at Romeo, who seemed to shrivel under her gaze while she took the last few drinks from me, leaving me with my citrus soda.

Juliet had finished handing out the food. With a small bow of the head and a muttered, "Enjoy." She quickly hurried out of the lobby.

"She seemed nice," but the tone with which Livia said it was acerbic, bitter.

"Yeah," *what else was there to say?* I

quickly turned to address all of them. "Listen, I just had a run-in with Tybalt. We need to be careful—" I was cut off by Romeo.

"We know, we saw him, too."

I stood still, taking a moment to process what my friend had just said. If they had seen him, then he probably had threatened them as well.

"You did?"

"Uh-uh," Romeo nodded.

"Well?" I asked giddily, too curious to express with words, "What did he say?"

"Nothing much," Romeo continued, throwing a piece of popcorn into the air and catching it with his mouth. The loud crunching that followed only stretched the answer he was about to give, and I felt my hands tighten around the bottle in my hand.

"He didn't see us," Romeo finally continued, "We stayed outside until he and his friends had gone."

I let out a deep sigh of relief. *Thank God Tybalt had not spotted them all together.* Montagues? And his cousins? *Imminent death.*

"So, did you see the girls with him?" I asked curiously, inclining my head.

"And the boys," Mercutio piped in. "There are three of them. One has really nice abs."

When I looked at him, he was smirking

[38]

up at me from his slouched position on the beanbag. Suddenly, he tilted his head to his right shoulder and lowered his gaze. His hand dug into the pocket of his leather jacket to reveal a glistening light-pink phone.

*I personally think it's pink*, mind you. But to be fair, it's the cover of the phone, not the phone itself, that has this noticeable color. Also, to be even more fair, or fairer, the cover is mostly white, but it has this glittering hue to it that somehow makes it seem to be a very light and very pale pink color.

Mercutio informed me it's a fairy dust phone, and the color is called 'champagne pink.' *Right.*

"Here. *Seeing the screening of the new Babes and Blunders movie with my crew.*"

I looked at him in surprise, then dove forward to peer over his shoulder at the screen of his phone. "Where did you find that?"

"I follow his accounts," Mercutio admitted with little shame.

"You do what?" At least I wasn't the only one who asked that question. Rosaline was with me. She stood on the other side of Mercutio and peered over his shoulder as well. We could hear how Livia joined her.

"Calm down, guys. It's just a bit of fun," Romeo interjected. He was the only one not bothering to come and take a look. *Which made me highly suspicious*.

"You follow him online, too?" I asked. But my friend's shrug was enough to confirm. "My God, how did I become friends with you two dumbasses?"

"Hey," Mercutio made it sound like he was offended, but the smile on his face told a tale that was quite the opposite. He held his phone a little higher for us all to see. "I only follow him on TikTok and Instagram."

The photo on the screen showed Tybalt surrounded by the girls I had seen earlier, plus a fourth girl who hadn't been at the counter. There were also three guys standing next to him, exactly like Mercutio had said. *Eight Capulets.* I gulped. That number was a bit too high. *We had to be really careful here.*

I squinted my eyes to study the abs of one of the Capulets. His flimsy red see-through sailor shirt revealed a lot of the magnificently trained shape he was in. I groaned and shook my head.

"All right," Mercutio pondered, "and I might have become friends with him on his account here."

The image he held in front of us left no room for doubt. "That's the most popular social media site to exist," Livia stated flatly as if this wasn't a big deal. "Everyone has an account on there."

[40]

"But they are friends!" I exclaimed. My cry of indignation was drowned out by Rosaline's words as she shifted next to me.

"Not everyone is on there," she huffed, eyes firmly focused on Romeo. But as she looked at him, I knew we were all thinking the same. Rosaline did have an account there. It's just that she's had Romeo blocked on social media for a while now. *Who would be the first to tell him?*

"Eh, right," I stammered, then slowly straightened my spine as I rose to my full height once more. "Shall we head inside?" I offered, thinking that it must be the safest. For all we knew, one of Tybalt's friends might decide to pop to the loo before the start of the movie and catch us all cluttered together. *That would be terribly inconvenient.*

"Yeah, probably a good plan," Romeo conceded. He pushed himself away from the wall he'd been leaning against.

"While there's still plenty of choice with the seating arrangements?" Livia piped in. Which reminded me…

Before they could enter the room, I stretched my arms to stop them, drink and popcorn still in hand. "Oh wait!" My box of popcorn ended in front of Mercutio's chest, who halted with a giggle. But as a result, everyone held still.

"Let's not take the front seats. Let's sit in

the back," I tried, knowing my voice wavered as I suggested it. I just hoped that no one had caught the slight quiver of fear in there. I didn't want them to ask what had happened or why I was adamant about sitting in the back row.

But luckily, no one asked. And apart from a curious glance from Mercutio, no one seemed to have second thoughts about my suggestion.

Livia led us to our seats, and I was relieved to find that the theater was already dimly lit. I followed her quietly, keeping my eyes on the crowd as we passed by. The Capulets were sitting in the middle of the room, closer to the front than the back, chatting among themselves and currently unaware of our entrance. I had to admit those were good seats they had chosen, but I was glad that we still had the back row to ourselves and a healthy distance between us and Tybalt's crew.

As we sat down, I looked to either side of me. Livia was on one side, and I expected Rosaline to join me on the other. But somehow, our solid seating arrangement seemed to have changed, and to my side, I found Mercutio's warm body as he laughed at the still-empty screen, pointing with a handful of popcorn and then stuffing it in his cheeks.

I could see the Capulets in front of us stir at the slightly too loud and very unique sound of

Mercutio's laugh. Vaguely, I discerned how Tybalt turned his head and narrowed his eyes. But luckily, just then, a line of people stepped in front of us, blocking their view of us. We no longer saw them either.

As the youngsters in front of us discussed their seats, I glanced at my row. Next to Mercutio, I found that Rosaline was unfortunately joined by Romeo. *This was not ideal.*

I groaned.

How am I supposed to survive a movie like this?

# *Two*

**"M**an, that was wicked."

The end song hadn't even finished when Romeo tried to approach Rosaline, leaning over to breathe down her neck. She quickly rose from her seat and made her way out of the room. All of us followed, with Romeo trying his best to reach her side.

"Yes, a disturbing plot," Mercutio agreed, having spotted the attempt and coming to Rosaline's aid by swiftly squeezing himself in between the two. I have to admit I admire him for that.

I was a few paces behind them, with Livia by my side, and I could not help but smile. Perhaps we had survived the movie after all.

"Not quite what I meant," Romeo sputtered, "but…"

"I think it is degrading for girls to be presented like that," Rosaline said, earning a heavy, consenting nod from Mercutio next to her. At least her brazen opinion had shut Romeo up, and I snickered, perhaps a tad too loudly.

"You don't agree?" *Ouch*, Rosaline's punch was directed at Romeo, humiliating the poor boy even further. If he said he did not agree, he would be making such a bad impression. *Not that he hadn't already.*

[44]

Once again, it was Mercutio who stepped in to help a friend. But this time it was to save Romeo from embarrassment.

"Hey, can you step aside? I need to pee." He pretended he couldn't squeeze past them to get to the loo, effectively interrupting their conversation and separating them. By the looks of it, Romeo believed him and took a step aside, pardoning himself. Rosaline just rolled her eyes and made a hasty step in the other direction, putting a healthy distance between herself and Romeo.

I smiled at Mercutio when he glanced at me from over his shoulder. His gaze silently told me that it was up to me to keep the two separated until he had returned.

*I would have loved to, but when nature calls…*

"I'll come with you, Mercutio. I need to empty my bladder as well," I could hear myself say the words, and I could see the disappointment on Mercutio's face. If he wanted to play it this way, then he had to sway. I *really* needed to *go*.

But then I saw it.

His eyebrows furrowed, and his frown deepened. There was a certain desperation in his eyes, and I realized it had not been an excuse. It was real. *Well, darn.* Who was going to protect Rosaline from Romeo now?

[45]

"And here I thought it's always the girls who clutter together," Livia said with a barb. I knew she blamed me for leaving the two of them alone with Romeo. And who would not? Romeo already had that scheming glint in his eyes.

"You're talking about Mercutio and me," I retorted, squeezing my own hand in an attempt to keep myself strong and composed. I was in no mood to explain myself. This conversation needed to end. Soon.

"And as far as we all know, he's half a girl himself," I said, pointing to Mercutio ahead of me. "If not three-quarters."

"Hey!" Mercutio shouted, already rushing toward the door to the men's room. The girls would have to sort this out on their own.

"Wait up!" I called out, not able to keep things under control for any longer, and I chased after him. Out of the corner of my eye, I saw how Livia attempted to sit on one of the ledges that connected the room to the hallway, but Rosaline intervened by gripping her arm tightly.

"What are you doing?" I heard Livia ask.

"Well, I need to go as well," Rosaline's reply came almost instantly. It was clear she didn't want to be alone with Romeo. I had noticed how he had been making unwanted advances toward her during the movie, placing his hand on her leg in a not-so-subtle manner. He was as tactless toward women as he was

[46]

smitten with them. It was painful to watch.

Upon entering the men's, we found that all urinals except one were taken, and we awkwardly stood in the back.

"Why don't you go first?" Mercutio suggested, his voice remarkably gentle. How very gallant of him. I looked at him and saw how calm he appeared to be. His eyes were resting on my hands, which, as I only noticed now, were trembling. "Yours seems to be more urgent."

And right he was. Friends like him are the best. The ones who let you go first in a line at the urinal. I took the opportunity and gratefully started to empty my bladder when the door opened behind me, and in came Tybalt.

*Of all people.*

He was on his own and looked a bit too smug once he spotted Mercutio. I could see it all happen in the mirror that hung in front of me. *Why did they hang mirrors here anyway? It wasn't very hygienic.*

Another spot had come free, and Mercutio, huffing as if he had not a care in the world, came to fill it. I could see the fuchsia-colored head in the mirror to my left, two men between us. He zipped open his tight jeans and pretended to ignore the Capulet. But he had no such luck. The spot next to him came free, and as if by purpose, Tybalt came to fill it up. The two

[47]

stood together, side by side, *in a urinal*. There was no way things were going to end well.

And I was right. Things went downhill when their shoulders bumped into each other. Not just a gentle or accidental push, but a forceful and blunt slam from Tybalt's shoulder into Mercutio's smaller one.

"Hey, watch it!" Mercutio yelped, his eyes darting at the mirror in front of him to meet Tybalt's malicious smirk.

"I'm sorry," the Capulet replied without sounding sincere, "I assumed you would have joined your girlfriends in the ladies."

*Girlfriends, huh?* Inwardly, I smirked at Tybalt's almost jealous-sounding insult. It was true that Mercutio often hung around with girls. But Tybalt's attempt to either degrade him by comparing him to a girl, or by suggesting he was someone who liked whoring himself out to girls, was rather pathetic. The girls I knew were all fierce and strong in their own way. Clever as well. To be compared to them or to be sleeping with them could only be seen as a compliment when it came from a man like Tybalt. No doubt Mercutio wasn't bothered by the insult either. Just offended that the Capulet had started talking to him.

Mercutio growled. "What sick suggestion is this?"

I was done in the meantime and tucked

myself away. It was awkward on so many levels, but I felt I had to approach them and break them up. Tybalt's suggestion wasn't even a bad one. Mercutio would be much safer going to the ladies at this point than staying where he was, next to the enemy. *With his junk on display*.

"Ah, nothing sick," Tybalt murmured, and the sudden change of his tone made me freeze to the spot. "Just a bit presumptuous of me." The Capulet's eyes drifted toward me in the mirror, a silent warning for me not to interfere. And I, indeed, stood frozen, unable to move. Perhaps I could say something to stop the two? But Tybalt's eyes had slid down, and Mercutio had noticed. The usually unashamed teen now had his cheeks turn red and fumed.

"When I said *watch it*, I did not mean for you to *perv down there*!" he shouted.

The other men at the urinals now started to interfere and I took my cue. I quickly turned away from them to wash my hands, knowing Mercutio would follow in an attempt to get out as quickly as possible. I was right. Within seconds, Mercutio had joined me at the basin. He looked displeased, and his lips curled downward as if he smelled something foul.

"Let's go," I told him, not wanting to spend a moment longer in the presence of the enemy. After drying our hands, we made a mad dash for the door, hoping we would reach it before Tybalt could get to us. I took pleasure in throwing said door shut in his face. The muffled curses of the other men scolding Tybalt for his inappropriate behavior made their way through the solid wall, and with a smile, I turned toward Mercutio. *That problem had been taken care of.*

My friend was looking at me with wide eyes.

"He grabbed me!" he said, louder than would have been appropriate. And as if to accentuate his point, he grabbed both of my upper arms in the process. "He grabbed me!" he repeated.

"Yes, yes, I heard you the first time. Now, let's get out of here," I urged him. Tybalt could emerge any minute now. Luckily, Mercutio's grip slackened, and I could shake his hands off. I took him by the wrist and started to pull him away from the danger zone.

In the corner to our right, I could see Tybalt's entourage waiting for him. They had spotted us and were clearly contemplating what to do. But I wasn't willing to wait around and see.

"Come on, Princess," I dragged Mercutio around the corner, and to my relief, we walked into the others. Romeo, Livia, and Rosaline stood waiting in front of a giant movie poster for *Grease*. Upon seeing us, they frowned, noticing something was amiss.

"What's wrong?" Rosaline asked, always the sensible one.

"No time to explain," I started while I handed Mercutio to her. "But Tybalt *manhandled* him."

I wasted no time and started our retreat. I took Livia by the arm and tugged her along while I reached for Romeo with my other hand. Rosaline was already dragging Mercutio, who, for once, did not object to the treatment.

"Manhandled?" Rosaline cried in disbelief as we made our way back to the entrance of the building.

"I can't tell you how *literally correct* that term applies to the situation," the victim, Mercutio, replied with a lopsided smirk while she dragged him along. "But he has *pleasantly* big hands."

The girls and Romeo 'ewed', and I knew exactly how they felt. *Big hands?* Had Tybalt seriously gone as far as to grope my friend? I was only too happy once the doors came into view, and I knew that the fresh night air was waiting for us outside.

The sky was dark when we emerged from the movie theater. Many small stars twinkled high above our heads. It was a clear night. Cold but not unpleasant. The chilly air cleared my mind, and for a moment, I closed my eyes and enjoyed the fresh air. Goosebumps

[51]

formed on my skin, and I relinquished the feeling. It made me feel so very alive.

Then reality hit and I could hear Rosaline's voice, urging us to head home. She was right, there was no time to stand still. Livia led me into one of the alleyways, where we waited for the others to catch up with us. Once they had, Rosaline turned to peer around the corner to look back at the movie theater. But she then quickly spun around to face us and pressed her back flat against the wall.

"They're coming," she said, her breath rapid and her eyes large with fear. In the darkness of the night, I could see the whites of her eyes. She was scared.

"Did they see us?" Livia asked worriedly.

"They certainly have seen us when we walked out of the restroom," I said, remembering the threatening glances Mercutio and I had received earlier. I felt Livia's hand warm upon me, her fingers curling tightly around my arm. I could hear Mercutio's shallow breaths. He was a couple of feet away from me and tried to peer around the corner to see if he could spot the Capulets. "Chances are high they saw us head in this direction."

A loud, uncharitable curse escaped Rosaline's lips, and she kicked her foot against the wall behind her. Her hands had formed into fists, which she brought up to her head as

[52]

she groaned angrily. Romeo attempted to step closer to her, but she held out a hand to signal him off. He luckily obeyed and stopped in his tracks.

"This might be over," she said, her voice bitter and her eyes directed at me rather than at any of the others. "If they know that we are hanging out, they will stop us from meeting up with you. We can't be friends with Montagues."

"No," the word escaped Livia without a thought. But upon realizing her voice had been a tad too loud, she quickly reduced her volume to a whisper. "No, we can't have that."

I could feel the way she was pulling at my arm, desperate to hold me close, unwilling to yield to fate. "Don't say that, sister," Livia said to Rosaline. "They might not have seen us, in which case we are in the clear."

"Well, they will see you if we keep dawdling here for much longer," it was Mercutio's voice that broke the conversation, and we all turned to look at him. He was peering around the corner, focusing on the movie theater just a street away. "They are breaking up, but I doubt they have forgotten about us," he added.

His alarming news had us all on edge again. "You mean, breaking up as in... forming search parties?"

"Several," Mercutio replied with a click of his tongue. His eyes were glued on the

Capulets, a sight we could not see.

"If they split up to find us," Romeo worriedly said while running a hand through his hair, "and they do, we'll be in big trouble."

"They will spot us as a group," Rosaline said. "I think it would be best if we split up as well. Livia," she turned to her sister, who reluctantly let go of my arm. "You're with me."

"Yes," I added, my mind racing. "That is for the best. If you two are found together and they haven't seen you with us tonight, then you might be able to talk your way out of it. Now go!"

I hardly needed to say it twice. Rosaline instantly dashed further into the alley, but Livia spun around on her heels to throw her arms around my neck, pulling me into a tight embrace. In it, I could feel the fear, and I closed my eyes and returned the hug. It was what I would have done for any of my friends. I wanted to give her all the courage and warmth and everything she might need from the embrace to strengthen herself for whatever was to come. And when we parted, I could see her look up at me in the dimness of the night. The whites of her eyes shimmered, and her teeth glinted as she smiled at me.

"See you soon," she whispered.
"See you soon," I whispered in reply.
And then she was gone.

I felt his eyes burn into me before I turned to face him. Mercutio was standing there, his head tilted, and his eyes narrowed. I couldn't decipher the expression within them.

"What?" I asked, feeling confused and slightly uneasy by the way his eyes glinted in the dark. *So full of emotion.*

"All right, the girls are heading south," he merely said, ignoring my question. "Which means we can't take the canopy road, which means we are left with Glamour Lane where the drag queens get their gear, or the one past old Mister Giovanni's home." Only Mercutio could use descriptions like that. "I opt for Glamour Lane. They have some neat-looking bathing suits on display."

As he said it, he turned to me, looking for leadership. I knew both routes he described, and with a small smile, shook my head.

"This is the plan, all right? We stick together. All three of us. No breaking up unless we really must." I turned fully to Mercutio and raised a finger. "And we don't go past Glamour Lane, no matter the fashion on display. We go via the old train station." He huffed in protest but followed my lead anyway.

Romeo was by my side while we made our way out of the alley. Rosaline and Livia would have gone right at the next junction, so we had to go left. Ahead of us, everything

[55]

seemed quiet. Normal. Behind us, we could hear sounds.

Some of the Capulets had followed us.

*No wonder.* They might be mean, but they were not stupid. Of course, they knew we would be walking home. They knew where we lived and how to get there. They could even take a different route and wait for us at our houses. A thought that made me shiver.

In the end, what chance did we stand?

"We'll make a detour, stretch it a bit until they grow tired, then head to our homes," I whispered, watching the slight movements of my friends as they nodded silently. "You know, just in case…"

Like thieves in the darkness of the night, we silently made our way across Verona. We used the alleys as our cover, obscure roads as our cloaks, and silence as our companion. Eventually, the voices behind us died down and we became braver, thinking we were all alone, and started to share jokes that became louder and louder. We were no longer followed. Surely not, or we would have noticed.

Then came the point where we parted.

"You sure we don't need to walk you home?" I asked Mercutio, whose house was only a block away now.

"Nah, I think I can handle it," he said with a smile.

[56]

Behind him, the sound of a trash can wobbling broke the silence of the night. I looked over his shoulder but saw a cat run away.

"Thank you, handsome gentlemen," Mercutio continued, capturing my attention fully, "for escorting me home." As he said it, he jumped toward me and flung his arms around my neck. The hug he gave me was similar to the one I had received from Livia, but it felt so much warmer. I took pleasure in hugging him back. I was laughing when I had to place him back on his feet.

"Good thing you're such a lightweight." I joked.

He winked at me, then turned to face my cousin. "And thank you, too, Prince Montague." Mercutio stood tiptoeing to place a kiss on Romeo's cheek, and I felt mine go red at the sight.

"Seriously, why did he deserve the title of 'prince'?" I asked when, in all honesty, the question I wanted to pose was, 'Why did he get the kiss?' I wasn't jealous. Not really. Just a little.

Just *a little much.*

Mercutio chuckled. "Because you're both princes," he clapped his hands together joyfully, "you're both *Charming.*"

*Wait, what?* While I thought about what he said, Mercutio gave me a quick pat on my shoulder before he ran off.

[57]

"See you, my men!" he shouted. The light from the streetlamps reflected on his black leather coat, illuminating the name of Montague. And with a giggle, he was gone.

I turned to face my cousin and we smiled at each other.

"He is so weird," Romeo said with a chuckle. I could hear the affection in his voice.

"Yes, but that's why we like him," I reminded him, and I could see I was right. Mercutio was dear to us both, a friend we did not want to live without.

"Shall we?" It was Romeo who now led the way. Smiling, we walked down the street, the long brick road stretching ahead, its tiles shimmering under the dim glow of the streetlights. There was a comfortable silence that hung between us as we walked. It was only broken when my cousin hummed.

"After seeing *Babes and Blunders*, I would like to see the prequel, *Babes and Plungers*."

I nearly choked. "Really?" That sounded like crap. "I don't think that would charm Rosaline much."

Here, Romeo halted to look at me with a smile and punched my shoulder playfully. "Hey, you're lucky," he said, "You have Livia eating out of your hand."

The visual image that was stirred did nothing to soothe me, and I realized I was scrunching my nose. Romeo laughed at my discomfort.

I frowned. "Isn't it rather the reverse? Mercutio keeps reminding me how Livia can play me. According to him, I am *easily* influenced," and as I said these words, I realized this was the truth.

"I do things because she says I need to do them," I continued, turning to my cousin with wide, frightened eyes, "Does she play me like a puppet? Have you noticed?"

Romeo just smiled sheepishly at me and rubbed his hands together. I was reminded of the fact that he had forgotten to bring his jacket along, and I shook my head whilst grinning.

I rolled my eyes to the sky and let out a loud sigh. We were nearing Romeo's home now. Already, I could see the vague contours lit by the many lights surrounding the windows and decorating the outline of the roof.

I raised my mobile phone to check the time.

"Hey," I started, intending to ask him what he'd be doing today. *Yes, today.* It was already past midnight by now, so the term *tomorrow* wasn't quite right to use, not in my opinion. The digital numbers were still flashing on the otherwise black screen when an eerie feeling took hold of me. It was like ice shards had formed in my gut, and I doubled over.

[59]

"What's wrong?" Romeo was instantly by my side and gently pried the phone out of my fingers to tug it into one of his jeans pockets. Once he had made sure my phone was secure, he put an arm around my waist to help me up.

"It can't be the drinks," he said, trying to be helpful.

"I don't know," I answered truthfully while I felt the cold feeling ebb away. The pain had been instant, but luckily, the duration had been short. There was only an awkward churning inside of me now. It was a feeling akin to fear. *Irrational but deep fear*. My eyes flew up to Romeo, who was smiling back at me. Then they wandered to peer over his shoulder at the alley behind us.

No one had followed.

"I suddenly have a bad feeling about this night."

"You think it's the girls?" Romeo asked, but I shook him aside.

"Not particularly, no." I just had this gut feeling, and it wasn't good. "I don't think they are in danger."

Romeo's thoughts finally caught up with mine as his eyes traveled to the empty alley behind us. "Then... Mercutio?" he hesitated, but his words were my thoughts.

"No," I quickly said, shaking my head, "it's probably just stupid." Mercutio had been

[60]

nearly home when we dropped him off. That corner had been his last obstacle.

*But we hadn't seen him making it to his house, had we?* What if they had been waiting in front of his door? His uncle owned a house with a driveway. They could have been hiding underneath the carport, jumping him in the dark when he brought out his keys to enter his home.

Romeo pulled at my arm, and despite feeling the chilliness of the night, he started to tug me away from his house and back in the direction of Mercutio's. "No way, man. If it means you can't sleep... We can head back, it's not a big deal."

I knew it was not a big deal, but it felt silly. Why should a feeling be taken seriously? Why? My thoughts interrupted themselves with more scenarios of doom. Now that I had started to think about the things that could have gone wrong, I imagined them getting worse and worse. The ominous feeling became heavier, harder to deny, and I allowed Romeo to drag me along.

We traced our way back, but this time, we did round the corner. The street we entered was eerily quiet. Tall houses stood on either side. This was one of the nicer parts of the city where those who had more to spend lived, as was obvious by the large houses looming over us in the dark. As we made our way toward

[61]

Mercutio's, a three-story high building, I could feel and hear little stones of asphalt scrunch beneath my feet. The feeling that something was off deepened. It became harder to breathe. The silence was deafening as we approached.

Romeo's arm shot out and I bumped against it, finding my footing with a silent curse. And then I heard it. Soft grunts. Mingled breathing. Someone was outside with us, and that someone was not alone.

I could feel my cousin's hands grab my arm now, pulling me away from Mercutio's home, but just by a few steps. I pushed back against him, bringing him to a stop.

And there he was. Mercutio. Pressed against the wall.

A figure was leaning over him, shushing him. But even in the dark, I could recognize the tall posture of Tybalt. And even in the silence of the night, I could recognize his voice when he grunted.

"We need to save him," I urged. My whisper came out harsh, panicking. I suppose we were in luck that the figures underneath the carport of Mercutio's house had not heard it.

But Romeo held me back. I looked at him from over my shoulder, accusingly, and wanted to ask why he delayed our rescue.

"I don't think he needs saving."

The words sounded foreign to me and I

could not understand them. But when I followed Romeo's gaze back to Mercutio, I could suddenly see. It took me a moment to let the realization set in.

Mercutio's arms were trapped next to his head. Tybalt's hands were curled around his wrists, keeping them locked. Their lips were engaged in a battle, as were their tongues.

Mercutio was kissing the Capulet. He wasn't just allowing it. *He was kissing back.*

I was speechless.

My throat had turned dry as I watched the two. My breath came out, shaking.

What was there for me to do? If we approached them, would Tybalt take out his blade? Would he try to kill us for walking in on them? But then Mercutio's soft moan reached my ears and I turned away, wincing.

"Yes, let us go," I whispered to my cousin, and then *I* took the lead.

Our journey to Romeo's, the same route we had walked only minutes ago, was one done in silent grieving. At least on my behalf. Romeo was uncharacteristically quiet as well, and when I glanced at him, it appeared as if he was thinking about something. That too seemed to be unlike him.

"I am sure we did right," I could not believe I heard myself say that. "If we had interfered…"

[63]

"Yes," Romeo cut me short, but I could hear that he forced himself to sound chipper when he actually was not. "Mercutio seemed to have it all under control."

"Yes."

Luckily, our awkward silence came to an end when we reached Romeo's house, and I led him to the door. I wasn't taking any more risks this night. Suppose one of Tybalt's fancy big men jumped out of the trash bin and grabbed my cousin. *Not going to happen.*

"So, this is where we part," I clumsily said, but there was so much more I wanted to say and found I could not.

Romeo smiled at me. "Quite a night, right?"

"Yes," I agreed lamely, "quite a night..." And one that I desperately wanted to forget. Eager to get to my own bed, I took a step forward and hugged Romeo tightly to me. He had unlocked the door and was already half-inside, standing with one leg over the threshold. "See you tomorrow."

He chuckled and returned the hug. "Take care, okay?" His voice was gentle, and I could feel him run his hand down my back like a silent encouragement. It was his way of saying that I needed to watch out. I was almost home, but not entirely, and he was clearly worried about me.

"I will," I said with a smile while I took a

[64]

step back from him. "Don't you worry."

With a false smile still on my face, I turned on my heels and made the first steps away from his house. The uncanny coldness inside my stomach was still there, but it had not worsened. As I walked, I pressed a hand to my abdomen and took a deep breath, willing the nauseating feeling to go away. I was only several feet away from Romeo when I felt it. *The worst feeling of all*. Something was blocking my windpipe, depriving me of the chance to breathe.

I reached for my throat and started to cough. Something was stuck, which was odd. I hadn't eaten since we'd seen the movie. Had there perhaps been a bit of popcorn stuck between my gums?

"Ben, are you all right?" Romeo came rushing to my side, but I waved him away with my hand.

"Go back," I managed to say between coughs and chokes. "I'm fine, just—" and like that, it came out. I coughed it right into my hand. But in the dark, I could not see what I was holding. Like a reflex, my hand curled around the obstruction and, as I caught my breath, I looked up to see Romeo at an arm's length away from me, hesitating.

"Go back inside the house," I said, this time in a normal voice. Romeo let out a sigh of

[65]

relief. "Must have been the popcorn."

He seemed to obey and turned away from me. "Now I remember why you're not a big fan of popcorn," I could hear him smile. "Be careful, though, and get home safe."

Knowing he could not see it, I stuck out my tongue at his retreating form before calling out, "I will," and then turned to continue on my way home. My fist loosened. Whatever had been stuck in my throat now dwindled out of my hand and onto the cold road below.

*In hindsight, I suppose that was the first petal.*

# *Three*

Mornings at Laurence's Footwear were usually quiet and relaxing. I could lose myself among the rows of polished shoes, the scent of new leather, and my daydreams.

But today was different. Today, the musty air was thick with the residue of last night, and every shoebox felt like a casket for my gloomy thoughts.

I couldn't shake the mental image of Mercutio laughing while Tybalt emerged from the dark, his tall body looming over him. Surely, it must have gone like this? They had been hiding in the shadows, secretly kissing. The memory left my heart pierced by shards of confusion and dread.

Why would Mercutio, with his colorful personality and his wild spirit, find himself entwined with someone like Tybalt? Had Tybalt threatened him?

Then again, Mercutio was the only one who had ever won a fight against Tybalt, it seemed unlikely he could be forced into this. Even if Tybalt was known for his creative threats.

*He was enjoying it. He was kissing back*, my mind unhelpfully reminded me. I didn't want to dwell on that memory, but I could not shake it off.

I couldn't help but wonder what happened after Romeo and I left Mercutio on his own. *We should have been there with him, guiding him to his door, then none of this would have happened.*

I felt guilty, even though I was well aware that Mercutio didn't seem to be in pain when we secretly spotted him in Tybalt's arms. Quite the opposite by the looks of it.

To make matters worse, Mercutio had never been a prettier sight. Flushed cheeks in the darkness, hoarse moans of pleasure, quiet begging for more.

*How I wished I had been in Tybalt's place.*

"Hey, Benvolio," Laurence's voice rang out, pulling me from my dangerous thoughts. I should not think such things about Mercutio. He's my best friend. Nothing more.

"These just came in. Could you get them up on the shelves?"

"Sure," I said before I had even seen the tower of shoeboxes that needed stacking. It would be a good distraction. The cardboard scent of fresh packaging filled my nostrils, overpowering the musty smell of leather and glue.

But even as I worked, my thoughts kept drifting back to Mercutio, his sharp wit, his boundless energy, his unexpected moments of vulnerability. There was an ache within me that I couldn't define, a yearning tangled with fear and something else, something that fluttered in my chest whenever he was near.

It was loyalty, perhaps, or maybe it was the beginning of loss. Would he start dating Tybalt after this? Would he leave us, his Montague friends, after Tybalt had won him over?

Was I afraid to lose my friend?

The soft jangle of the bell above the door yanked me from my task, a stark reminder that the world outside continued to spin, regardless of the tempest within me. I glanced up, half expecting another random customer. But no, this was no ordinary visitor. My eyes widened at the sight of a familiar face.

"Good morning, Ben, my boy!" Mercutio's voice boomed through the store, catching me by surprise.

"What are you doing here?" The words spilled from my lips without a thought. Mercutio loved to sleep in. It was rare to see him at this early hour. Unexpected even, especially after last night. Normally, you couldn't get him out of his bed. Not on a weekend day.

*Suspicious…* Had he even slept at all?

"Well, now," he said, faking that crestfallen look that he could put on so well. I swear, he could have made a proper actor. The

[69]

girls would love him. *Boys as well.*

"Aren't you happy to see me?"

I blinked, confused. "Of course, I am happy to see you."

"That's what I thought," Mercutio said audibly, wiggling his finger teasingly. With cheeks flushed red, I instantly looked around the store, taking a deep breath of relief when my boss was nowhere in sight. There seemed to be no other customers who had seen or heard Mercutio's teasing.

"Quit it," I whispered, embarrassed, causing Mercutio to laugh out loud at my expense.

"Mercutio," I murmured. "Shut up. Anyway, you're lively for someone who..." My words trailed off, a memory of last night's shadows playing at the edges of my thoughts. *Him,* trapped against Tybalt's body.

"It's Saturday," Mercutio exclaimed with a flourish, unaware of the thoughts occupying my mind. As if the day of the week explained away the dark circles that should have been under his eyes.

"Right. It's Saturday." I echoed his statement, but it hung between us, laden with unspoken knowledge. *Exactly.* What had the dawn offered him that sleep could not?

"Free as a bird on Saturdays," he chirped, spinning on his heel to parade down the aisle

[70]

between the shelves. "Thought I might come and annoy you for a bit. How about I try and buy some of these hideous shoes you have on offer? Like those ladies you always complain about. Trying them on, strutting around whilst complaining they aren't the right color, then placing them all in a pile before they head home without buying anything."

I watched him, perplexed by the lightness of his steps and the ease of his grin. Then, I shook myself out of my thoughts while I followed him hastily down the aisles. Too late, apparently. He had already stopped in front of the women's shoes and picked out a box.

"Seems about my size," he muttered, though I wondered if it really was. Mercutio was by no means tall, but his feet weren't small either.

"Hey," Mercutio's voice cut through my contemplation once more. "Next time we go to the movies, I'll pick one. Yesterday's one was about as funny as a funeral."

"Misogyny wrapped in a cheap joke," I said dryly, the corner of my mouth lifting despite myself. "Typical Romeo choice. The guy lacks tact."

But we still loved him. I just held hope that Romeo would grow out of it one day and become more serious.

Mercutio chuckled while he pulled high-heeled pumps out of a box and kicked off one of his own sneakers. A purple sock with a hole at the toe became visible, and I noticed how my eye darted to his foot. The way he wiggled his toes was entrancing.

"He really lacks tact, yeah," he agreed as he sat down on the little square chair in the middle of the aisle. He then tried to squish his foot in the high-heeled shoe with little success, despite the wiggling.

"I think you should go for a bigger size, Cinderella," I muttered, earning myself a squinted glare from my friend. But Mercutio finally relented, and as he went on the hunt for a bigger size, I let out a deep sigh.

"Fetch me my glass slippers, oh prince of shoes," Mercutio mocked, but I grinned and shook my head.

"You can pick them yourself," I watched him pull out another box from the women's section. *Red pumps. Nice.*

"Next time, we should go for something like a romantic comedy," he suggested, voice smooth like honey. I ran a hand through my hair while I watched Mercutio make a mess of the boxes I had just neatly been stacking. *Seriously?* It seemed he was going to make true on his promise, picking out shoes randomly and trying them on, then sighing and placing them in a pile in the middle of the aisle.

[72]

"Mercutio, for God's sake," I complained, but it only earned me a snicker.

"What, I am bored," Mercutio whined playfully, turning to face me as he pulled out a different box.

"Who do you think has to clean up all this mess?" I grumbled, though I couldn't truly be angry with him. Mercutio in high heels was rather a sight to behold. *Though I wouldn't tell him that.*

"I'm just making sure you won't have to be bored either," Mercutio said with a fake pout.

My eyes darted to the door of the employer's room. My boss was still out of sight. Thank goodness for that. If he saw the mess Mercutio was making, he'd probably flip his lid. I sank to my knees to pick up the first few pumps, browsing the shelves with my eyes to see where they came from.

"Ben," Mercutio called out, that familiar lilt in his voice pulling at my attention like the moon coaxing the tides. "What's your expert opinion on these?" He held up a pair of garish sneakers, their neon colors clashing horrendously with the royal blue denim of his jeans.

"Unless you're planning to guide ships through fog, I'd steer clear," I quipped. My heart was beating fast, too loudly. I hoped he couldn't hear. I was actually enjoying myself, grateful that Mercutio was making my dull morning that much brighter with his presence and silly jokes.

"Ah, but they say the brightest stars are often the most fleeting," he mused, placing the sneakers back on the shelf only to pick up another pair, this time a set of formal oxfords. "Perhaps something more classic? What do you think, Benvolio?"

"Classic doesn't suit you," I murmured. "I'd return to the red pumps."

Mercutio stuck out his tongue. "Joker," he said. "Red doesn't match my fuchsia hair."

I rolled my eyes while I collected some more shoes in my arms and pressed them tightly against my chest. If I hurried, the pile could be gone before Laurence returned from his break.

"Right, because you are the fashion expert," I said. "Didn't you once tell me that you could make everything work?"

"Everything suits me," he retorted, a devilish grin spreading across his face as he sauntered over to the mirror, the shoes forgotten. He preened like a peacock, winking at his reflection before turning those deep, brown eyes back on me.

"Wouldn't you agree?" His voice was silk, wrapping around my reason, tugging gently until it unraveled.

"Mercutio," I started, the name catching in my throat. The fantasies that flew into my mind were too many and too rich. *Yes, he could wear almost anything he wanted and get away with it.* At least, *I* thought he could get away with it. But the thoughts I had weren't the ones you had about friends. If they had been, then my heart wouldn't be racing right now, and my cheeks wouldn't color. I also wouldn't have dropped the shoes I was holding. With a silent curse, I bent to pick them up again.

"Ah, forget it," Mercutio said with a dismissive wave, stepping away from the mirror and heading toward the door. "I should let you work. And besides, I've got places to be, people to dazzle."

"Of course," I managed, the sound barely above a whisper.

He paused at the threshold, casting a glance back that felt like the sun emerging from behind clouds, a warmth that filled my chest, spiraling out until it reached my fingertips.

"Bye, Bennieboy," his words drifted to me, as did the imaginary kiss he had blown my way. And then he was gone.

A sudden pain pierced my chest and I hunched forward, pressing a hand against the sore spot.

How could the warmth inside of me transform this quickly into pain?

Something rose in my throat, and I frowned, waiting for the feeling to subside. Once

[75]

it did, I bent over again to pick up the shoes and managed to collect them just in time before my boss returned. I flashed him a careful smile the moment he saw me, my arms still filled with shoes. He merely raised a brow.

"One of them ladies again?" he asked, and I nodded.

"Yeah."

*Mercutio had played the part well.*

Time crept along the walls of the shoe store like a weary shadow, stretching and contracting with the fickle morning light that filtered through the front display window. Now that Mercutio had gone, the store had grown quiet again.

I tried to focus on the rhythmic motion of stacking shoeboxes, each one a hollow chamber echoing with unspoken words. I should have said something about catching sight of the two of them. I should at least have tried to discover whether he actually felt for the Capulet or if this was just some fling.

*Why hadn't I?*

[76]

I tried to keep my mind distracted. Several elderly couples and a few moms with young kids visited in the morning. The scent of new leather and polish lingered in the air, offering a familiar comfort with each sale. As the day wore on, the store grew busier, and the questions that had weighed on my mind began to fade. I was darting from one customer to the next. By the time the store was crowded and I'd almost completely forgotten about last night's events, a familiar voice suddenly called out to me.

"Hey, Benvolio."

Livia Capulet stood behind me, an impish smile curving her lips. Her hair was a chaotic symphony of bleached and red strands, her coat slightly unzipped as she shuffled from one foot to the other.

"Hey you," I greeted. I'd almost forgotten it all, and now everything came rushing back. *What was wrong with me?*

"You're going to love this," she announced, her eyes glinting with a secret triumph. "We got away clean last night. Tybalt's been sniffing around, playing bad cop with Rosaline and me, but he's clueless about us hanging out with you Montagues."

My heart skipped a beat. I wished it was from relief, but the truth was I saw them again in my mind's eye, entwined in shadows. *Just when I had finally begun to forget.* The memory surged back at full force and I had to push it aside. I was surprised that Tybalt still had the energy to go around interrogating his cousins after his late-night encounter with Mercutio yesterday.

"Tybalt always did have more brawn than brains," I remarked dryly, hoping my voice didn't betray how shaken I still was by yesterday's events.

Livia leaned against the counter, her gaze roaming over my face as if searching for something hidden beneath the surface.

"You know," she said, her tone playful, "you were really brave yesterday. I know how rough my cousin can get, and I know Tybalt threatened you. Yet, you got us out in time, came up with a brilliant plan, and shook them off our trail."

A flush crept up my neck, the compliment settling awkwardly around my shoulders like an ill-fitting cloak. Because I *hadn't* shaken them off our trail, had I? Tybalt had managed to corner Mercutio. Of course, Livia didn't know.

Oblivious, or perhaps indifferent, to my discomfort, Livia reached out to brush a stray curl from my forehead, her touch light but laden with intent.

"Always there to keep us out of trouble," she continued, her voice dropping to a murmur.

"So brave, so... *handsome*."

*Wait a minute.* I shifted under her gaze, feeling something heavy settle inside the pit of my stomach. She didn't really mean that, did she? She wasn't… coming onto me, was she?

"Livia," I began, already aware of how pitiful my voice must sound. The idea that Livia liked me, that she romantically liked me, frightened me. I needed to find a way out of this conversation before it became too awkward. Maybe I could use work as an excuse? It was busy enough for that. Behind her, customers gathered, eager to pay for their new shoes.

*Unlike the 'flirt' that had been fitting on every woman's shoe his size earlier this morning.*

*No, I had to stop thinking about him.* Why did he keep drifting to the front of my mind? I was here now, working. I had to focus on my job and Livia.

"You give me too much credit," I said, hearing my own forced chuckle. "I am just a guy who works in a shoe store." And here I gestured behind her. "And I don't want to chase you away, but there are customers who need me."

I turned to the woman who stood behind her. "Can I help you?"

The woman smiled and greeted me, then placed her chosen shoes on the counter. Livia didn't seem discouraged.

"Oh, you're too modest, Benvolio

[79]

Montague," she teased, though the sparkle in her eyes had dimmed. She stood a little more to the side and watched as I helped the customers, one by one.

"Perhaps," I conceded, my voice barely audible over the clamor of my own conflicted emotions. When the line of customers kept growing, Livia let out a sigh.

"I'll catch you later, Ben. Mom has taken us out for a drink and a bit of shopping. I can't stay away for too long without a viable excuse."

I grinned. "You could always tell her you wanted to buy some new shoes. We've got some great red high heels here. Your color, I swear. Or some neon sneakers."

Livia let out a soft laugh. "I bet, but if she sees me talking to a Montague, she'll probably cause a scene. It's safer if I just leave."

Was that a hint of sadness I saw on her face? Surely not, right? Then again, something inside of me was telling me that Livia had read more into the two of us hanging out than just a simple friendship.

"See you around, Benvolio," Livia said softly, a hint of wistfulness in her tone as she leaned in closer. An expectant pause hung heavy in the air. *Perhaps I hadn't misread her words earlier after all.*

I could see the intention in her eyes, the subtle tilt of her head inviting what I knew I could not return. As her arms reached out, beckoning for an embrace that might have culminated in a kiss, a sudden lurch within my chest seized me. My breath hitched, and without warning, I doubled over, my hands clutching at the counter for support.

"Sorry," I gasped between spasms, the word tearing from my throat as though it were lined with thorns. "There's something—my throat…"

With a startled step back, Livia's arms fell to her sides. "Benvolio?" Concern etched her features, replacing the softness that had been there moments before.

"No, it's okay," I managed, straightening up while fighting the urge to cough, the tightness in my chest like cruel roots entwined around my lungs. The world seemed to tilt, reality blurring at the edges. "I'll be fine."

Her brow furrowed, but she nodded, casting one last lingering look. I gave her an encouraging smile, wishing her to leave.

"If you say so," she said, though I could hear the doubt in her voice. A new customer placed their shoes on the counter in front of me, and I forced a 'good day' from between my lips. Apparently, it was enough to convince her that I was indeed fine enough. She hesitated, but then she blissfully turned and walked away.

I staggered, clutching at the counter for

support, breaths coming in short gasps as I helped the customer. Once they had gone, I doubled over, a silent scream lodged in my lungs, and from deep within, I felt the rise of something weird and tangled, a foreign feeling I had never felt before. Except perhaps yesterday?

It was a bit similar, but whatever was in my chest, whatever threatened to rise like bile, felt more cluttered and more tangled than yesterday. Bigger. Only, I hadn't eaten any popcorn this time. I hardly had eaten at all this morning.

I waited until the feeling faded, and slowly, it ebbed away. But not in time for my boss to have noticed. I felt Laurence's concerned gaze upon me.

"Benvolio," he began, his voice tinged with a paternal concern that seemed to fill the small store. "You're looking peakier than a ghost in moonlight. Are you sure you're doing all right?"

I attempted a reassuring smile, though it felt like a flimsy attempt. "Just a bit under the weather, I guess."

"Under the weather, he says," Laurence muttered, shaking his head as if he could dislodge my ailments with the gesture. "Look at you, all pale and shaky. You need rest, not a day spent with shoes and difficult customers."

He clapped a hand on my shoulder, its

weight somehow grounding. "Go home, Ben. We'll manage here without you."

"Laurence, I—"

"None of that now," he interrupted, ushering me toward the back with a gentleness that betrayed his gruff exterior. "Off with you. And don't come back 'til you've got some color in those cheeks."

I nodded, too weary to protest. Perhaps Laurence was right. Perhaps all I needed was a good night's rest and then the queasiness would go away. I wondered if it would also help me forget everything else. Tybalt embracing my best friend like they weren't sworn enemies. And the look Livia had given me.

I wish I could forget both.

# *Four*

The cursor blinked relentlessly, a silent metronome marking the end of my academic torment for today. I leaned back in the chair as a soft sigh escaped my lips, eyes stinging from the glare of the screen that had been my companion for hours on end. Laurence had told me to go home and get well. But sitting around or lying in bed for the remainder of the day felt wrong. Mostly because I felt normal again, okay enough to do things. And my hands were aching to get some work done.

I wasn't ill. I could convince myself of that. Perhaps I'd eaten something wrong yesterday. Perhaps the popcorn had been off. *Can popcorn be off?*

The walls of my room seemed to close in on me. I was lucky to own a student room in a shared apartment in the middle of Verona. But at the same time, that meant I only had this one room to myself. Perhaps I could go outside? Have a change of scenery? All other areas of the house weren't private, and I didn't fancy interacting with any of my roommates.

A dull throb nestled between my temples. It was not quite painful enough to be a headache, but persistent enough to remind me of its unwelcome presence.

[84]

Like I said, *I wasn't ill.* This was just... because I'd been behind my computer screen for too long. Yes, that was it.

I pushed away from the desk, stretching limbs that felt as though they'd been molded into the shape of my chair. My mind wandered, yearning for something or someone to break the tedium. Grasping my phone, my fingers swiped across the smooth surface with practiced ease. I scanned the messages for Mercutio's name. He was somewhere at the top of my list, but there had been no new messages since I last checked. The last one had been a winking emoji blowing a heart. I could send him a message, I suppose. But perhaps I should lay off him a little, see if I could forget everything if I gave it a little more time.

I sighed and scrolled. Lots of Montague nonsense. A few messages from my parents. But it was Romeo's name that flashed atop a mountain of notifications, a beacon of drama in the mundane sea of social media updates.

*"Can you believe it? Rosaline says we're done!"* his message read, the words dripping with a desperation that was all too familiar.

"Done?" I mused aloud, thumb hovering over the keyboard. "Were you ever truly begun?"

I could send a message like that, saying that there had never been anything between them to begin with. But that would be rather harsh. And would it solve anything?

Rosaline had never even wanted him. I wondered if Romeo had truly been this blind all along. I truly wanted to see him happy. But come on. Rosaline wasn't the one.

My response was tender despite the thoughts turning in my mind.

*"Romeo, she was never yours to lose."*

Send.

A simple message, yet heavy with the weight of unspoken counsel. Romeo, bless him, with his sun-kissed hair and chiseled abs, always leaping before looking, plunging heart-first into the shallows and mistaking them for depth. I suppose the girls would call him a womanizer. I suppose I should call him that as well.

He would charge headlong into another love, another loss, and I would be there to pick up the pieces, as always. Nothing new there. I just hoped the message had finally come across and that he would leave Rosaline be for a while. God knew she needed the breather. We all did.

A wave of weariness washed over me as I awaited his reply. It wasn't just the assignment that had drained me; it was this ceaseless cycle of comfort I provided as naturally as breathing. Yet somewhere beneath the fatigue, a spark of protectiveness flickered. After all, wasn't that what family did? Stand by each other through

[86]

the frivolous and the grave?

The silence of my room, thick with the stillness of a stagnant afternoon, was broken only by the idle tapping of my fingers on the phone screen. I scrolled through the endless parade of status updates and selfies, each one a reminder of lives moving forward while mine seemed caught in a perpetual lull.

A vibration against my palm pulled me from the reverie as a message from Livia popped onto the display, her words punctuated by little hearts and smiley faces.

*"How are you feeling, Ben?"* it read, her concern bleeding through the pixels. But today, her affection felt like a shackle I wasn't ready to bear. Since I realized that she might see us as more than friends, well… I figured I had to become a bit more hesitant in my approach toward her. With a flick of my thumb, I swiped the notification aside and submerged myself back into the digital stream, seeking distraction from thoughts I dared not entertain.

As I skimmed past the usual cacophony of cat videos and political rants, Rosaline's page caught my eye. A wry smile tugged at my lips as I read her latest post: *"Tybalt decided he'd be the world's biggest pest this morning. #SomebodySaveMe."* It was just like her to air family laundry with such casual humor. Intrigued and craving more of this familial soap

[87]

opera, I clicked the link to Tybalt's profile. Would the message show on his page?

But the moment the page loaded, my smirk froze into an expression of shock. There, glaringly prominent amidst the slew of photos and ego-fueled gym check-ins, was a status update that screamed for attention. *'It's complicated,'* it said, the words standing out like a red flag on a battlefield. My heart thumped erratically against my chest. Complicated with whom?

*It's complicated.*

It truly isn't, I thought, heart beating fiercely in my chest. My mouth turned dry. His relationship had been updated in the early hours of this morning.

Unbidden, the image of Mercutio's face surfaced in my mind, his smile as enigmatic as the Cheshire Cat's, stirring a warmth within me.

*It's complicated. Right?*

I feared it could only mean one thing.

A post beneath it sent a jolt through me, Emilio Capulet—had he been with the group of them yesterday?—had left a comment that tied my stomach into knots.

*"Wishing the best for you and Mercutio."*

My eyes scanned the words again, refusing to comprehend.

Mercutio? *My Mercutio?*

A torrent of emotions cascaded through

[88]

me, betrayal and confusion waging war with the loyalty I felt toward him. The room spun slightly, and I gripped the edge of my desk as if anchoring myself to reality. Questions formed like storm clouds in my mind, each one darkening my thoughts further. How? Why? When?

How long had this been going on? I always thought they were enemies, not lovers. That couldn't have just changed overnight, could it? Had their midnight meeting not been the first time they had been close? Had Mercutio kept his relationship with Tybalt a secret? From us? From me?

*Had he lied to me?*

With hands that trembled ever so slightly, I dialed Mercutio's number. I had not even given it a thought. It just happened. Each ring echoed in my ears, a countdown to a truth I wasn't sure I wanted to face. Surely, this was all a bad dream.

"Hey, Benvolio!" Mercutio's voice erupted through the speaker, as vibrant and carefree as always, unaware of the turmoil that roiled within me. His tone was happy, yet it did little to ease the tightness in my chest. I steadied my voice, a practiced calm masking the tempest inside.

"Mercutio, we need to talk."
Silence. Well, that was

uncharacteristically for him. My dread increased. But then, just as I thought the world had come to an end, he laughed. That carefree, wonderful laugh of his.

"Ben, sweetheart, spit it out. If it's about Rosaline and Romeo, I already know, and I had nothing to do with it. If it's about the gum on the silver stiletto shoe, that was just a joke, but I won't apologize."

He rattled on, just as I was used to, and I breathed a sigh of relief. So he already knew about Rosaline and Romeo's scuffle today. Romeo must have told him, just like how he had messaged me. *Good.* And the silver stiletto… "I—wait, what?"

Mercutio's loud laughter filled my ear. "Oops, forget what I said. I'm sure Laurence won't kill a pretty boy like you for it. Tell him it was another difficult lady customer."

I groaned. When had he done that? I had been watching him like a hawk this morning when he was in the store. Right?

But then, the matter that occupied my mind the most spilled forth. No sugarcoating it, no disguising it.

"Mercutio, what's this about you and Tybalt?" I asked, my voice threading a line between casual inquiry and veiled urgency. The room felt too still, the air around me holding its breath as I waited for him to unravel this knot

[90]

tightening in my gut.

"Tybalt?" Mercutio chuckled on the other end, the sound of it usually enough to send warmth flooding through my veins, but not today. "He's just a storm in a teacup, Benvolio. Why? What have you heard?"

*Right,* I thought cynically. A teacup Mercutio wanted to press his lips against? A storm he was happy to consume? *Was that it?*

I hesitated, the words teetering on the edge of my tongue. I wanted to press, to ask him to reveal to me what happened last night and how long this had been going on.

Instead, my resolve wavered, the stark loyalty I bore him clamping down on my curiosity.

"Nothing concrete," I replied, attempting nonchalance while my heart raced against my ribs. "Just some odd social media posts that caught my eye."

"Ah, the vile beast of online gossip," he said, his tone light, dismissive. "Pay it no mind, Benvolio. People love to stir up drama where there is none."

His assurance should've been enough, but doubt lingered like the last note of a song played in a minor key. I listened to the cadence of his laughter, the rhythm of his voice, searching for a discordant beat that would betray the truth. But there was nothing. Perhaps this was the truth?

I realized then that pushing him further would only erect walls between us that I wasn't willing to build. So, I swallowed the unasked questions.

"All right," I conceded, allowing the lilting timbre of his voice to wash over me, soothing the jagged edges of my fears. "Just making sure you're okay."

"Always am, with you looking out for me," he teased, a smile in his words that echoed in my chest.

We talked of inconsequential things then, his latest fashion exploits, the antics of a stray cat he'd befriended, anything to reweave the normalcy that had so suddenly frayed. Our conversation took over an hour, but it felt as if only minutes had passed. And when we finally said our goodbyes and I looked at the clock, I realized it was nearly time for dinner.

The sun had already dipped low on the horizon, its rays tenderly caressing my room. A silence fell over me, heavy and introspective. I sat alone amidst the quietude of my room, letting the remnants of our conversation settle within me. The angst that had clawed at my insides ebbed away slowly, leaving a bittersweet relief in its wake.

Mercutio was still Mercutio. My friend. *My Mercutio.* Did I really just think that again?

What was wrong with me that my thoughts of him had suddenly become more possessive? He was his own man, his own person. *He wasn't mine.* Yet, I liked to think of him as such. What did that mean?

But more importantly, I trusted him. Had to trust him. If he said that Tybalt was just stirring drama, then that was only what it was. If it hadn't meant anything to Mercutio, then I should trust him that it hadn't meant a darn thing.

And still, my heart hurt. Why? He could do his own things.

*He isn't mine.*

I stood, limbs heavy with fatigue that was more emotional than physical, and shuffled toward the kitchen sink, hoping the splash of cold water on my face might help me think clearer. The faucet coughed into life, spitting out a reluctant stream that caught the light in prism-like droplets.

I cupped my hands, gathering the chill of the water, and splashed it against my skin, seeking solace in the shock of its touch. But as I straightened, a convulsion seized my throat, making me lurch over the basin. My body heaved with a rough, wrenching gasp, and from my lips, a single pale petal fluttered into the stainless steel void below.

A petal. Soft, delicate, and undeniably

real.

My heart hammered a frantic tempo as I snatched it up, the cool, velvety texture incongruous against my trembling fingers. It was pink, a shade so soft it seemed to hold within it the last whispers of a sunset long faded. How? My mind raced, hunting for logical explanations where none could exist. *A petal? From my mouth?*

My apartment held no flowers like this. I scanned the room just to make sure. Mercutio liked to tease me for being a *'plant dad'*—or whatever that meant. I just liked plants. But I didn't have any with these pink petals.

I'd been indoors for hours now.

Fear prickled at the base of my neck, spreading its icy tendrils down my spine. Had this truly come from me?

I glanced around my apartment one more time, just to make sure. I had a few plants but no bouquets or blossoming arrangements. Nothing that could shed such a beautiful petal. It must be a figment of my imagination.

But the petal lay in my palm, tangible evidence of the absurd. The faint scent of it teased my nostrils, a fragrance that spoke of hidden places, of secrets kept in shadow. My chest tightened around the breaths that now seemed shallow and insufficient.

*What did one do with a mystery wrapped in a*

*petal?*

I let it fall, watching it dance briefly in the air before it joined the other forgotten castoffs in the trash. It must have come from somewhere, I reasoned. And it meant *nothing*, I told myself.

I turned my back on it, trying to ignore the creeping dread that sought to take root within me. I busied my hands with the familiar task of preparing dinner.

As the knife sliced through vegetables, the rhythm of the blade against the cutting board was a mantra that banished the impossible. Hearing the sizzle of oil in the pan and smelling the aroma of spices blooming in the heat, I slowly started to relax.

A good meal would fix things. Because, like I said, *I am not ill.*

Or so I wanted to believe.

# Five

The steady rhythm of raindrops against the café window provided a musical soundtrack to my waiting. It had been a couple of days since I'd last seen Rosaline, but we had agreed to meet for a drink. Just to have a chat and distract our minds a little.

Mercutio still hadn't spoken to me about Tybalt. Romeo seemed to ghost me. Livia was livid. And my chest still ached.

Things could be better.

I stared out of the window as I waited for her. Tiny spheres of water trickled down the glass, a beautiful sight and entertainment of its own. I watched as the raindrops seemed to chase each other down the glass and tried to predict who would win.

I had tried to keep my rest the past few days and take everything slow. I still had that weird chest ache, and sometimes it felt like something was clawing inside my throat, trying to find a way out. A weird cough had lingered. But that was all. I convinced myself I was on the mend.

"Hey, you've been hogging the best view," Rosaline's voice, light and teasing, cut through the fog of my thoughts as she slid into the seat opposite me. Droplets were caught in

[96]

her hair like dewdrops on a spider's web. Her smile was a beacon in the dimly lit coffee shop and infectious. I felt the corners of my mouth twitch upward.

"Only the best for you," I replied, gesturing at the small table already cluttered with my half-finished mug of tea and a scattering of napkins. *Okay*, so the napkins were a decent way to keep from coughing all over the place. But I am fine, *truly...*

She shook off the dampness from her coat. "Can I get a large cappuccino, please?" she asked the barista, before turning back to me, her dark eyes scanning my face with a concern that was both appreciated and slightly unnerving. "How have you been, Ben? Livia told me you were ill. You look... better?"

"Ah, yeah, I think so," I said, attempting to sound more convincing than I felt. The remnants of my illness lingered like a shadow, but it wasn't something I wanted to dwell on.

"Good," she nodded, accepting my answer with a hint in her voice that betrayed she was wishing for my speedy recovery. She glanced outside, watching the rain with the same fascination I had moments ago. "I love the rain. It's like the world is starting fresh, don't you think?"

"I suppose," I murmured, lost for a moment in the beauty of the rain sliding down the glass.

"Ben?" Rosaline's voice pulled me back, her hand reaching across the table, a gesture meant to ground me. "You're doing that thing where you get lost in your head again."

"Sorry," I said, giving her a small smile to reassure her everything was fine. "Just thinking. It is beautiful out there. I've never really minded the rain. I know others do."

"Others like me," Rosaline said with a chuckle. "I don't like getting wet."

I raised a brow at that comment.

"You just said you love the rain," I know my voice skipped a notch. But I like to pretend it didn't. My reaction earned me a chuckle from Rosaline, who shook her head.

"I love seeing the rain. But I don't like getting wet," she clarified. I had to think about her statement for a minute, as it sounded so contradictory. Then I relented.

"Well, if I ever become an inventor, I shall invent an umbrella with two parts. One that shields you from the rain, and the other with a big, massive hole for me."

She laughed at this, and I couldn't help but chuckle along. The idea was silly, but that is exactly why I had voiced it out loud.

"Always the dreamer," she quipped, the warmth in her tone taking the edge off the worry that still lingered in her gaze. "It's one of your better traits, though."

"How do you mean, one of my better traits?" I challenged, grateful for the shift back to our easy banter. "I thought all of my traits were the best."

"Now you're sounding just like Mercutio. Is he infectious?" she asked with a smirk. And I felt my tummy do a little flip at the mention of his name.

"Wish it were so. We could do with a bit of his jolliness."

She laughed, and I couldn't help but join in. The sound mingled with the soft patter of rain, creating a harmonious blend as the barista served Rosaline her drink. The steam from her cup curled up like whispered secrets, disappearing into the hum of the coffee shop. Once our laughter had died down, I took another sip of my tea, the warmth slowly filling me.

"Ben, if I may ask... how are you and Livia?" Rosaline's voice was tinged with concern. She watched me over her cup, her eyes sharp and searching.

I hesitated, the words catching in my throat. "She seems to be mad at me," I finally admitted, "because I didn't reply to a message quickly enough."

I watched her closely for her reaction, but I could tell by the serious glint in her eyes that she was already aware of this. Of course, being sisters, Livia must have told her. For a moment, I worried that Rosaline's real reason for inviting me was to talk about her sister. I hoped not. I was still contemplating how to break the news to Livia that I just wanted to be good friends with her, nothing more. It wasn't really something I ever had to do before.

"Truth is, Rosaline, I think she has the wrong idea about us," I finally said after worrying my bottom lip for a long while. The gentle smell of ginger and mint drifted by, easing some of my nerves. My hand tightened slightly around my cup before I rolled my shoulders back, easing my muscles. "I never meant to give her that impression."

Rosaline nodded slowly, her lips curving into a knowing smile. "I've suspected as much. Livia isn't your type, Ben. You need someone who understands the quiet spaces inside you."

Relief washed over me like a gentle wave. "You noticed?"

"Of course," she said, her tone softening. "And Livia, well, she's angry right now. She's been talking about marrying you for so many months." Here, Rosaline rolled her eyes, like Livia had been tiring her with talk of this. But I sat frozen and blinked, wondering if I had heard her correctly. *I hadn't, right?*

"And suddenly, you stop giving in to her

[100]

every whim. Which, I think, was a good move. She just had to prod you with a stick, and you would dance for her, so to speak. Not replying to that one message got her riled up." Rosaline swirled her hands elegantly through the air as she talked, the words spilling from her lips at a rapid pace. I had difficulty keeping track of what she said.

"I think she had been picturing a marriage between the two of you, thinking it could end the feud between our families. She already picked out a dress and everything…"

My heart stuttered, shock jolting through me as though I'd been drenched in cold water. This time, I knew I had heard her correctly. "Marry me?"

"The whole table arrangement, who should be invited, and where it should be held. *Oh,* and she wanted a carriage with white horses," Rosaline continued, only falling silent when she saw the perplexed expression that had to be on my face. "Yeah, I know. I think it was all a bit much as well," she finally concluded, not sure how to interpret my silence.

"She wants to marry me?" I was pretty sure my voice skipped a notch. "That's…"

"Insane?" Rosaline offered, a laugh escaping her before she could catch it. Her hand flew to her mouth, eyes widening in apology. "Oh, Ben, I'm sorry. It's just so ludicrous."

[101]

I shook my head, trying to wrap my mind around the absurdity of it all. "No, you're right. It's completely absurd."

She sat a little straighter in her chair and circled her hands around her cup, her eyes intently on me.

"I know, Livia can be a bit," she seemed to be searching for the right word, "*obsessive*." Her gaze was sympathetic, yet firm. "But don't let her tell you how to live your life. Also," here she clicked her tongue, "you have me. I've got your back in this."

I was quiet for a moment longer, letting the words settle into the fogginess of my brain. I'd only recently started to realize that Livia saw me as a possible *boyfriend*. And now I heard she already considered us to be official enough to plan an entire *marriage*? The thought creeped me out.

"I, I don't know what to say," I looked at Rosaline and saw her lips curl into a smile. She held her cup a little tighter. "T-Thank you?"

"You don't have to say anything," she said, a playful glint in her eye. "Although I would have loved to have you as my brother-in-law."

Here, I scooted my chair backward with a loud scraping noise, the panic obvious on my face. My palms were open wide, hands still pressed against the edges of the table between

[102]

us. "Now, hold on!"

"I do," she interrupted me. "I do like you quite a lot. So much, in fact, that I will shield you from my own sister," here she sighed and her eyes softened. I felt myself calm down somewhat as I watched her shoulder sag. "You're too good for this world."

I blushed. I could not help it.

"You're a cinnamon roll," she whispered.

*What a weird compliment.*

"Is that a good thing?" I asked, the corner of my mouth lifting despite the turmoil within.

"Definitely," she affirmed with a nod. "Though I wouldn't mind if you became family, I can see you don't love Livia. She isn't your type by far," she said knowingly. "We at least have that in common. We're not like… most people, are we?"

A comfortable silence fell between us.

The rain continued its gentle symphony against the coffee shop windows, a soothing backdrop to our conversation. The sound was punctuated by the occasional clink of metal against glass as people stirred their drinks, and the soft hum of the espresso machine as it exhaled steam like a slumbering dragon.

"I am glad I have met you," I mused, turning my mug in my hands, "and I am glad Romeo finally gave up the chase."

"Absolutely," Rosaline replied, her eyes

[103]

sparkling. "Hopefully, I no longer need to worry about him."

I nodded, watching raindrops running down the window's glass, when a familiar figure outside caught my eye.

"Speaking of worries," I said, hesitating. "Isn't that Romeo?" I gestured subtly toward the window.

Rosaline leaned forward, peering through the glistening curtain of rain. "You're right. Well, he moved on quickly after he finally got it through his thick skull that I am not interested in him," she gestured exasperatedly with her arms.

"Which Mercutio and I have been telling him for ages," I added.

But Rosaline was already leaning over the table and squinting her eyes. "Who's that he's with?"

Now it was my turn to squint my eyes as I studied the two figures frolicking in the rain.

"I recognize her," I said, a hint of surprise coloring my tone. She was the girl from the movie theater, the one who'd helped me carry the snacks and drinks. "Wasn't she called Juliet?"

They sat down in front of a café across the street, sheltered under a wide awning. Romeo leaned in, his smile possessing the same magnetism that seemed to ensnare hearts

[104]

effortlessly. Juliet, her attention entirely captured by him, laughed—a soundless echo through the glass—and tucked a strand of hair behind her ear. *They were flirting all right.*

"Look at them," Rosaline whispered, a touch of something unreadable in her voice. "They're in their own little world."

"Seems so," I agreed, watching as Romeo brushed his fingers across Juliet's hand, a gesture that spoke louder than words.

Romeo's laughter, a distant chime, carried through the glass, and Juliet mirrored him with a grace that seemed almost fragile. But her laugh once again remained silent, not loud enough to beat the rain and the barrier between us.

I felt Rosaline's gaze upon me. In it, I saw a worry woven with an unspoken plea.

"Should we... warn her?" she murmured, her voice as delicate as the subject itself. "Juliet seems like a nice girl. She doesn't deserve to be just another of Romeo's passing whims."

I nodded, the weight of agreement heavy on my chest. "Yes, she seems kind. And undeserving of heartache. Especially from my cousin."

As we watched, Romeo cupped Juliet's face in his hands, their silhouettes painting a picture of untainted affection. The sight should have been touching, but it stirred a disquiet

[105]

within me, a restlessness that clawed at my throat.

"Ben?" Rosaline's concern pulled me back from the brink of my own spiraling thoughts. "You're looking pale."

"Am I?" The question left my lips before I registered the tightness in my chest, the subtle strain for air.

My breath hitched, a sharp inhale trapped by a sudden onslaught of coughs. I covered my mouth, hoping to quell the unwelcome intrusion. When I pulled my hand away, specks of crimson sullied my palm, a stark contrast to the creamy surface of the coffee shop table.

*Shit, not again*, was all I could think. My stomach constricted, and my throat hurt like hell. I had been doing so well. What could have triggered such a response? Was it something I ate or drank? Was it something in the air?

"Ben!" Rosaline's voice was edged with panic now, her hand reaching out to steady me, fingers cold and urgent against my burning skin. "I thought you said you were getting better?"

"Sorry," I managed between coughs, each one bringing forth more petals, tiny fragments of a blossoming dread. I looked at them in silent wonder. Where did they come from? Although I already knew the answer.

*Inside of me.*

[106]

But that was impossible. Unless I had swallowed a tree of some kind. I hadn't, had I?

I tried to push away my panic and quickly moved my hand, hoping that Rosaline wouldn't see the petals in my palm if I kept my hand curled as a fist. Then I dropped them out of her sight. The petals fluttered to the floor, a silent confirmation that I wasn't cured yet. But it was something I was desperate to hide.

"Let's get you some water," Rosaline suggested. She scanned the room for assistance, missing nothing, not even the way my gaze lingered on the couple outside, nor the way my hand had formed into a fist in front of my lips again.

The barista got me a glass of water, but I kept making noises as if I was choking. Rosaline's hand was on my back now, her touch both comforting and urgent as she tried to ease the spasms that wracked my body. Slowly, my body seemed to calm, but I felt tired and out of breath.

The door to the coffee shop chimed, a gentle intrusion into the rhythm of my struggling breaths.

"Have the two of you seen Romeo? He's here with," Livia's voice cut off abruptly when her eyes found me, contorted in discomfort, her sister's hand battering my back. "Ben, what's wrong?"

[107]

"Can you get some tissues?" Rosaline asked, her gaze never leaving mine, filled with a silent understanding of the turmoil I felt within.

Livia was the last one I wanted to see right now.

She was still angry. She was still expecting me to be her boyfriend.

*Good lord, I'd better not think of it.*

"Of course," Livia said, concern etching her features as she rushed to the counter, her bleached hair with the red strikes trailing behind her like a fiery comet against the cafe's tranquility.

I could feel Rosaline's eyes on me, sympathetic yet calculating. As soon as Livia was out of earshot, Rosaline leaned in closer, her voice a whisper meant only for me. "I didn't know she would come, Ben. I'm so sorry! I don't think the two of you together is such a good idea. Not right now."

"I know," I confessed, the words barely audible over another round of coughs. "I don't want to be with her, Rosaline. Not now."

"Then go," Rosaline urged, a determined glint in her eye. "I'll handle Livia. Just... take care of yourself."

Grateful for her protection, I nodded, gathering the remnants of my strength to stand. The world tilted slightly, but I steadied myself, knowing I had to leave before Livia returned.

[108]

With one last apologetic glance toward where Livia stood, oblivious to the conversation we'd just had, I skidded past tables and chairs, the murmur of the coffee shop fading behind me.

As I pushed through the door, the cool air hit me, mingling with the scent of rain-soaked pavement. I glanced in front of me to see that Romeo and Juliet were still caught up in each other's eyes. Grateful that they hadn't noticed me, I quickly rushed into one of the alleyways. They hadn't seen me, which was good. No one had to witness my inglorious escape.

I took a few more steps, and suddenly, there he was. A blue and pink smudge in the otherwise gray alley. A bit like the stray cats he adored.

It was Mercutio, in all his fuchsia-haired glory. He stood out like a burst of color against the dull afternoon sky.

"Ben?" His deep brown eyes were wide with surprise, concern quickly clouding them as he took in my disheveled state.

"Mercutio..." His name escaped my lips like a plea.

Of everyone I could run into, I ran into him.

# *Six*

Mercutio looked at me, wide-eyed, his appearance sudden and vibrant even beneath the dreary sky. His wet hair stuck to his forehead and his denim jacket was sticking to his thin frame, but despite being thoroughly soaked, he looked more like a god than a drowned rat.

The alleyway was a dim, narrow gash between brick buildings, filled with the scents of espresso and cinnamon from the coffee shops lining the street just beyond. I could almost taste the bitterness of fresh grounds on my tongue, mingling with the petrichor rising from the rain-soaked earth. Rain drummed a frantic rhythm against the cobblestones, like a thousand tiny fingers tap-tapping a code of urgency.

Mercutio turned fully toward me and smiled. Raindrops clung to his fuchsia hair, darkening the strands to a rich wine color. They trailed down his cheeks, which were flushed from the chill, and I couldn't help but think he looked inexplicably cute when wet, like a mischievous sprite caught in a downpour.

"Ben! How nice of you to drop by," he joked, but I caught the underlying concern. I raised a brow and had to suppress a smirk.

"Really, *I* dropped by?" I groused. "To meet you in the middle of a random alley?"

Mercutio huffed, and I shook my head with a chuckle. "Well, you ran into me, pretty boy," was his only defense. "Just saying."

I felt my cheeks blush again and quickly looked away. I knew I wasn't in the clear yet. Livia could catch up with me at any moment. I could only pray that Rosaline managed to keep her distracted for long enough to get me a head start. Nervously, I glanced over my shoulder, half-expecting to see Livia's shadow looming out of the gray.

"Rosaline and I... we had a meeting," I said, words tumbling out in a rush. "Then Livia showed up, and Rosaline... she covered for me. So I could escape." I paused. "Apparently, she wants to marry me."

Mercutio's eyes grew wide. Upon realizing what I had just blurted out, I backtracked on my own words.

"I meant *Livia* wants to marry me. Not Rosaline. Rosaline told me that Livia was fantasizing about wanting to marry me, and right now, Livia is super angry because I didn't reply to one of her messages swiftly enough, and now I can't do anything right," I rambled in one go.

"Seems you shattered that girl's dream there." A loud laugh escaped Mercutio's lips, and I watched him with a sense of despair. There appeared to be something carefree about his

[111]

posture all of a sudden, as if there had been a tension that was now gone. But I didn't give it much thought.

"That's not funny," I lamented, but Mercutio laughed anyway. He placed his hands on his hips and tried to straighten his spine.

"Ben, you're just as bad as your cousin." And I frowned because I didn't like to be compared to Romeo. But perhaps Mercutio had a point. It seemed that I, too, was skilled at breaking a girl's heart. I'd just never imagined it could be as easy as not replying to a message within five minutes after it was sent.

*Or an hour or three.*

I glanced at Mercutio. Should I tell him that it was our conversation that distracted me from answering?

Mercutio's deep brown eyes scanned the alley as if he, too, expected the specter of Livia to materialize from the damp shadows. There was an unspoken understanding in his gaze. Neither of us wanted to be confronted by Livia and her wrath. I could feel the tension coiling in my gut, the fear that she might follow, that she might be close enough to hear the pounding of my heart.

"Let's get you out of here," Mercutio said decisively, stepping closer. He offered a crooked smile that didn't quite reach his eyes, betraying his worry for me. "I've helped Romeo escape dates before. I can help you as well."

I suppressed the urge to roll my eyes, but was silently grateful that he offered to help me out. As he pulled at my arm, I fell into step beside him. The cobblestones glistened beneath us, reflecting the neon signs of the shops we passed.

"I saw Romeo on a date," I said as we quickened our pace. "With that girl from the movie theater. Juliet? They were... well, it looked like a successful date."

Mercutio's fake surprise was evident even under the brim of his soaked-through fuchsia hair. His eyebrows arched, a light in his deep brown eyes flickering with something akin to disbelief. "Really? How unexpected."

*Like I said, he is a good actor.* But I have known him for years. Judging by his reaction and the fact that he hung out in an alley nearby, he *must* have seen them. I glanced over at Mercutio and couldn't help but notice how the raindrops clung to his lashes, how they traced the contours of his cheeks. He was always so alive, so vibrant, but now he seemed part of the storm itself. Wild and untamed.

"Speaking of unexpected," I ventured, my voice barely rising above the patter of the rain, "what were *you* doing in that alleyway? Waiting for someone?"

My heart skipped, fear gripping me at the thought of Tybalt lurking nearby, watching us

[113]

with his predatory gaze.

*Surely not?*

Then again, Tybalt's status update flashed in front of my mind's eye. *It's complicated.*

Why did it still bother me so?

Mercutio's stride faltered for a moment, a flicker of something unreadable crossing his face before he mastered it with his usual nonchalance. "No, Benvolio, I wasn't waiting for someone. I didn't have a date, in case you were wondering. Unlike Romeo and *you*..."

*Wait?* Had it bothered Mercutio that I might have been on a date? Which I wasn't, *but...* The thought alone made my heart do a little jump inside my chest.

"I wasn't on a date!" I blurted out, only to realize that Mercutio had started to snicker before I had even finished my sentence. So perhaps I had misread him. Perhaps he had just been teasing me?

"Oh, you," I growled, but I couldn't truly be angry at him. "Anyway, if you weren't waiting for a date to arrive, then why were you—" I began, only to be cut off by his sigh.

"Okay, so perhaps," here Mercutio hesitated and eyed me, measuring my reaction to the words that were about to follow. He'd been up to something. *I knew it!*

"Perhaps I did know that you were going

[114]

to meet Rosaline there? And perhaps I did know that Romeo would see Juliet today. And perhaps I was deliberately snooping around town."

"Oh my God, I knew it," I gasped. I had been right all along. He had been following Romeo. "You were spying on them."

"Was not," Mercutio huffed while he folded his arms in front of his chest. I watched the tight fabric of his denim jacket hug around his muscles. "But," here he glanced at me and hesitated. "If I did, I promise I had good intentions," he said defensively.

He raised a hand, his slender fingers held up in front of me to shush me.

"I just wanted to be near, in case either of you needed to be rescued," his tone sobered.

I quirked a brow, giving him a sidelong glance as we continued our walk through the backlit alleys of Verona. The sky was turning darker. "What made you think that either of us needed rescuing?"

"Well, it seems that *you* just proved my point," Mercutio muttered with a grin.

My cheeks flushed again, and I gasped. *The audacity of him!* "I can't believe it…"

*But he was right.* I had been in dire need of a savior today, and I was grateful that my savior came in the shape of Mercutio.

We turned another corner. The cobblestones were slick beneath our shoes, and the evening air carried the mingled scents of espresso and petrichor. A symphony of dripping rain played offbeat to our hastened steps, and I felt the rhythmic pounding in my chest sync with the sound. Above us, the first stars were cheekily appearing, blinking down at us as the sky continued to darken.

"Easy there!" Mercutio's voice pierced the dimness as he stumbled, his foot jarring against a shadow that darted away with a startled mewl. It was a cat, its fur a patchwork of night and moonlight, eyes gleaming like two drops of mercury.

"Sorry, Snuggles," he chuckled, his laughter a warm balm against the chill of the rain. His hand slid into the pocket of his jeans to come out holding a cat snack. He bent down, extending a hand toward the creature. "Hey, come here, little guy."

I couldn't help but laugh along, watching the way his fingers wiggled in an attempt to coax the cat, *Snuggles*, closer. Trust Mercutio to know cats in Verona by name. For a fleeting second, the tension unwound from my shoulders, and the world was nothing but Mercutio, the cat, and the silent rhythm of falling droplets.

But then the night shattered with a sound more jarring than any thunderclap, a voice calling out through the dark. *Livia's voice*. Hadn't

[116]

we walked far enough? It was tinged with a possessive note that scraped against my nerves.

How on earth had she found us here?

"Mercutio," I whispered, the panic evident in my hushed tone. Had he heard her? It wasn't just in my head, was it?

"Time to run," he replied with a smirk, his eyes twinkling as they met mine.

I nodded, and we bolted like the wind, racing as fast as we could. The streets blurred into streaks of color, and the rain painted everything with a glossy sheen. The world reduced to the sounds of our breaths and the urgent beat of our escape. *Which was thrilling.*

It reminded me of when we were cheeky little kids and had to run away from angry adults, usually because of some prank pulled by Mercutio or Romeo. We did that thing where you rang someone's doorbell and then legged it. But we also 'borrowed' gnomes from people's front gardens, or those big ceramic birds that came in all the bright colors of the rainbow. I remember how Mercutio claimed he wanted to collect them, saying he 'loved birds, pun intended'—*what pun?* But in the end, he had to bring each and every bird back to their original home.

*Those were the times.*

"Keep up, Benvolio," Mercutio urged, always one step ahead, leading me through the maze with the ease of a man who knew every crack and crevice.

It was easy to see that he was experienced in parkour, with his long limbs and graceful strides. I knew he was deliberately keeping to the roads so I could follow rather than jumping up against a building and taking to the roofs. I would have loved to see him run like that. When he jumped from roof to roof, it was as if he were flying, as free as a bird. But I was grateful he kept to my side and stuck to the boring routes below.

I ran along, a big goofy smile still plastered on my face. I never felt more alive than when I was running alongside Mercutio.

His hand reached back for mine and I clasped it without hesitation. Our fingers entwined, and in that grasp was a promise, a vow silently spoken that he would not let me falter, that he would not let me fall behind. His hand felt soft and warm in mine, despite the coldness of the rain. *So alive.*

We ducked into another alley, a shortcut only known to those who favored shadows over light. My lungs burned with the effort, but Mercutio's grip was unyielding, his presence a constant force by my side. He pulled me after him, guiding me toward safety.

And toward him.

I tumbled against him, lips parted in a

silent gasp of surprise when he pulled me close until our chests were pressed against each other. Standing close, I could see the water droplets that clung to his lashes.

His breath, tinged with mint and some rebellious aroma that I could only assume was his own, kindled a fire within my chest. It wasn't the sprint through the narrow labyrinthine streets of Verona that left my heart doing acrobatics. It was the way his deep brown eyes seemed to capture the scarce light filtering in from above, turning them into wells of liquid chocolate, impossibly warm and inviting.

A strand of fuchsia hair had fallen across his forehead, and without thinking, my fingers reached up to brush it away. The hairs felt soft, like fine silk threads against my skin, a stark contrast to the roughness of his denim jacket.

"Easy there, Benvolio," Mercutio whispered, his voice low, sending a shiver crawling down my spine despite the closeness of our bodies. "You're safe now." His lips curved into that all-too-familiar mischievous smirk.

Before I even had the time to comprehend what was happening, he grabbed my wrist and started to drag me out of the alley again.

"I don't see or hear her any longer. I think we got away," he said, a chuckle escaping his lips. His fingers were still wrapped around my wrist, skin on wet skin.

The rain had dwindled to a delicate drizzle. As we stepped out of the alley, this time certain that we were no longer being followed, we couldn't help but laugh. Mercutio's hand slid from mine as he reached for his stomach, tears rolling down his cheeks.

"I need a breather," Mercutio gasped between fits of laughter, his eyes alight with mirth. "It's been a while since I saw you being chased, Ben, my boy. I, on the other hand, get chased all the time."

I couldn't help but chuckle, shaking my head at the absurdity of it all, our impromptu chase, our breathless flight, and the way Mercutio's hand had felt on my wrist, his fingertips pressed against my pulse.

It was a pity he had let go.

"You're terrible," I said, though my smile betrayed any semblance of reproach.

"Terribly charming, you mean," Mercutio countered, winking as he nudged me playfully with his shoulder. It was a simple touch, fleeting yet charged with something more, something unspoken that sent a warm shiver skittering down my spine.

We found ourselves walking now, our pace leisurely compared to the frenzied sprint from mere moments ago. The streets welcomed us like old friends, their familiar contours guiding our footsteps as we drifted away from danger and toward a sense of peace only found in each other's company.

"Mercutio," I began, hesitating. "Thank you, for... for everything." My gaze lingered on him longer than necessary, tracing the lines of water that still traced his features, oddly beautiful in their transient paths.

"Anytime, Benvolio," he replied, his voice soft like he was whispering a secret. "What are friends for, if not to rescue one another from the perils of unwanted admirers and stray cats?"

"Right," I said, smirking.

As we emerged from the alley, the city unfolded before us, the lights reflecting in the puddles like fallen stars. We dodged them playfully, each step a dance, each laugh a note in the symphony of the night. And as the rain ceased its song, leaving only the echoes of our joy, I reveled in the presence of the boy who danced beside me, the friend who seemed to chase away the shadows that clung to my soul.

"Race you to that lamppost," Mercutio challenged, his grin devilish as he pointed toward our new finish line.

"You're on," I agreed without a moment's hesitation, knowing full well he would win. As we ran, laughter spilled from us. This was ridiculous. We weren't children anymore. Yet, when we were together, it felt as if we truly were free. As if we could take on the world. That wonderous kind of feeling.

And still, I tried to outrun him. Fool that I was.

The laughter dwindled to a soft chuckle as I caught my breath, hands on my knees, feeling the dampness of the evening air cling to my skin. Mercutio was doubled over beside me, his fuchsia hair plastered against his forehead in a way that made him look wild and untamed. The neon lights from an open sign flickered in his eyes, casting shadows across his face and giving him an ethereal glow.

"Admit it," he panted, straightening up with that mischievous sparkle still in his eyes, "You let me win."

"Never," I breathed out, though the corners of my mouth betrayed me, curling into a smile.

Mercutio's phone buzzed sharply in his pocket, jarring against the quiet murmurs of the city around us. His hand darted to silence it, but not before his expression shifted. It tightened in a way that sent a prickle of unease down my spine. He glanced at the screen, and for a split second, I saw a shadow cross his usually radiant features.

"Everything okay?" I asked, concern lacing my tone. A part of me feared that this could be the end of our time together. It was probably selfish of me, but at this moment, I didn't want Mercutio to leave my side. I wanted to hear his laughter a little while longer.

Mercutio hesitated, his gaze flickering from his phone to meet mine. Then, with a deliberate motion, he slipped the device back into his pocket, the lines of worry smoothing from his brow as if they were never there. He offered me a smile, warm and reassuring, and my heart responded in kind, skipping a beat.

"Nothing I can't ignore," he assured me, and there was something fierce in the tilt of his chin, a silent promise that whatever called to him from that screen, it wouldn't steal him away from me. *Not tonight.*

Knowing this felt good, and I felt my chest swell with pride. He wasn't going to abandon me, still my rescuer as always.

"Good," I said, the word more a sigh of relief than a statement.

"Let's go over to your place," he said, that smile turning crooked and playful once more. "I'm not done with you yet, pretty boy. You're going to be stuck with me a little longer."

There it was again, that flutter in my chest. I laughed, the sound mingling with the distant murmur of the city, and nodded toward my apartment, a mere few streets away.

"Lead the way then," I said, stepping closer, close enough to feel the warmth radiating

[123]

from him in the cool night air. "My place isn't far."

"I can't believe you no longer remember where you live!" Mercutio gasped, his exaggerated expression of shock made me double over again in laughter.

"You idiot," I said between chuckles. "Of course, I still know where I live. I just meant that you know the way. And, as you have just so pleasantly proven, you're way faster than me. You're probably going to drag me to my own home."

At this, Mercutio chuckled. And was that a light blush I saw on his cheeks?

"I am not a Capulet dog, but, sure, I shall lead the way," Mercutio quipped, looping an arm around my shoulders with easy familiarity. "Besides, I got you all wet, and I heard you already have a nasty cough. I make an excellent nurse... among other things."

My cheeks felt heated as I melted into his touch. "You did not make me wet," I retorted, perhaps a bit too swiftly. He let out a laugh again while I mused about the other words he had said.

"And I am worried now," I said, raising a brow skeptically. "You, as a nurse? And what do you mean? Among other things?"

The feline-like grin that met my gaze was enough of an answer. "You're going to have to find out for yourself, Bennieboy."

## Seven

The skateboard screeched against the concrete as Mercutio pulled off yet another impromptu trick, landing with that same self-assured grin that never seemed to fade. I watched from the bench, my hands fiddling with the frayed edges of my denim jacket, a nervous habit. There was a ping.

His phone showed an incoming message. From *him*. Tybalt. And I didn't know how to address this fact.

"You've got a new message," I decided to say instead, keeping it vague.

Mercutio's eyes lit up as he stepped closer to look at his phone in my hand. But the light in his eyes faded when he saw Tybalt's name on top of the screen. His lips curved downward.

"Not who you had hoped it would be?" I asked.

"Romeo's gone AWOL on us again," Mercutio grumbled, not answering or mentioning Tybalt. He flopped down beside me, his hair a vivid fuchsia under the rays of sunlight. Was he hoping to hear from Romeo?

"Ever since he's been smitten with that girl, it's like we're just shadows to him," he grumbled.

I hummed. "It's always like this when he's madly in love. You know how he gets, blind to everything else." My gaze drifted across the park. It was a nice sunny day after all the rain we just had, and the park was brimming with life. Mostly teenagers, but also the odd elderly couple could be found. The sun made the air feel a little warmer, emitting a sense of peace that was accentuated by the rustling of leaves.

Mercutio stretched out, arms behind his head, and I couldn't help but notice how the sunlight danced across his features, casting half his face in light and the other in darkness. It was an ever-present reminder of the duality within him, the wildness versus the vulnerability.

"Speaking of love," I ventured, my heart rate picking up. I'd almost forgotten Tybalt and the 'incident'. *Almost.* "We know my cousin is having success. But how are you doing? No recent conquests?"

Something flickered across Mercutio's face, but it happened too fast for me to read it.

"None worthy of mentioning," he said, which made me frown. Because that wasn't what I remembered. An image of Mercutio in Tybalt's arms came to mind. But even though the incident happened weeks ago, Mercutio had never mentioned it to me or Romeo. And he had been by my side for most of the time since Romeo started dating Juliet.

I turned to watch Mercutio through squinted eyes, taking in his appearance. He seemed relaxed, a torn hole in the knee of his jeans showing some soft flesh underneath. I don't know why my eye was attracted to it, but I couldn't deny it. He caught my gaze and followed it, smirking.

"Like what you see?" he teased, and I instantly snapped my head to the other side, feeling embarrassed for having been caught ogling my best friend. Instead of entertaining him by playing along with his game, I decided to track back on our conversation.

"It's just that, you usually have a crush or two who want to date you," I carefully said, knowing that although Mercutio had been very out in the open and had been on more dates than I could count, he wasn't like Romeo in the slightest. If Mercutio dated, it was for the fun of it. *He was still searching*—those are his own words. But I didn't know if he was searching for someone to love, or if he was searching to find himself. Perhaps both.

"And you have been spending most of your time with me recently," I knew I flushed at this and quickly glanced away, too shy that he might see. Once I had composed myself, I looked back at him, full of expectation.

"Huh, so I have," Mercutio teased me, running a finger past my cheek and deliberately

[128]

tapping the skin until I blinked. We both laughed.

He leaned back on the bench and closed his eyes, basking in the early warmth the sun finally provided.

"Well, I can't help it if I am irresistibly handsome," he said, a grin plastered on his face.

I groaned again. He was either unaware of what I wanted to know or deliberately avoiding my unspoken question. *Were he and Tybalt a thing*? That was what I wanted to know but dreaded to ask. I'm pretty sure Tybalt had texted him that day he rescued me.

He moved his foot, the skateboard clattering against the concrete as it was lifted and then fell back down again. I sighed and decided to go for a different tactic. And this had to work, I reminded myself, because how more obvious could I get?

"Did you see Tybalt's status update? Said *'it's complicated'*. Sounds cryptic."

"Tybalt?" Mercutio scoffed, a hint of disdain flitting across his visage. "Who cares about what he posts? That guy's world is all smoke and mirrors."

"I guess," I said softly, feeling the weight of unspoken truths hanging between us. Was my best friend truly hiding a relationship from me? It felt like it had to be so. But Mercutio had always been honest with me. So darn honest, he

[129]

never had anything to hide. And he had been with me for most of the time.

Then again, he had been with us at the movies when we caught him in Tybalt's arms afterward. What had I done wrong that he felt he couldn't trust me with this now?

Was it because Tybalt was a Capulet? An enemy? Did he think I, as a Montague, wouldn't understand?

But Mercutio's denim jacket still spelled the name Montague in proud letters. He still hung out with me. He texted me every single day. Tried to involve me in his hobbies and other daily activities. Nothing had changed there.

So why would he lie?

"Speaking of being busy, your schedule is just as packed," I tried a different tactic. *Just tell me*, I silently begged. I didn't want to ask him straightforwardly, felt like I couldn't do that. As if the words wouldn't come out even if I were to try. *Show that you still care about me enough to trust me.*

"Parkour practice, fashion shows, social media... Don't you ever feel stretched thin?"

"Stretched thin?" He laughed, a sound that usually set my soul alight but now only deepened the shadows in my heart. "Benvolio, you don't need to worry. I've got all the time in the world for you."

[130]

His eyes met mine, deep brown pools reflecting earnest intensity.

"I am here now, aren't I?"

Heat crept upon my cheeks, a silent betrayer of emotions I kept shackled deep inside.

"But just for you, though," Mercutio said, a whispered afterthought. "I'm not going to share my time with anyone else."

I turned away, pretending to be absorbed by a pink petal that had found its way onto the bench between us. I frowned. It reminded me of the petals that I had been coughing up recently. Had this one come from between my lips as well? Had I simply not noticed?

I swiftly brushed it away with my fingers, hoping Mercutio hadn't noticed the stray petal, then looked around.

There were no trees from which it could have fallen.

"Thanks, Mercutio," I whispered, smiling at him while he smiled back at me.

"Not sure what you're thanking me for, Bennieboy, but you're welcome," he said, taking obvious delight in the way he had me all flustered.

For a moment, the two of us sat in silence, enjoying the blueness of the sky above our heads and the soft rays of light that warmed our skin.

Then, Mercutio shifted next to me. "Did

[131]

you use sunscreen? You've got to be careful with that skin of yours."

I rolled my eyes. "Oh my God, Cutio, I swear…"

"*Cute, I know*," Mercutio joked, and it took me a moment to realize he was creating a pun on his own name. I groaned and slapped his thigh playfully.

"Cut it out," I grumbled.

"Just worried about you, bro," Mercutio mumbled, his dark eyes resting on my face. But his expression was calm, tranquil. As if he were in thought.

"Which reminds me…Do you still need my services as a bodyguard? You know, Livia?"

I winced as that was not the topic I wanted to talk about today, but fair's fair. I've been trying to tear personal information about his life out of him. No wonder he was trying to do the same.

"Rosaline says Livia's been quieter lately," I said as casually as I could muster, picking at the seam of my worn-out sneaker. "Thinks she's got her eyes on some Capulet."

"Ah, the forbidden fruit has become less interesting at last." Mercutio's voice danced with amusement.

"I am *not* forbidden fruit," I snapped at him, only to see his brown eyes spark intensely.

"Aren't you?"

[132]

I opened and closed my mouth like a fish, my tongue suddenly feeling rubbery. *Just because of the Capulet-Montague feud…*

"You can't just take a bite out of me," I cried out, noticing how some of the kids nearby turned to look at me. Exasperated, I threw my hands up in the air.

"Fine, you win, Mercutio. I have just made a fool of myself. *Again*. But don't compare me to fruit, please," I looked at him with the fiercest gaze I could muster.

It worked, somewhat, because Mercutio leaned back against the bench in laughter and covered his mouth with his hands to quell the sound.

"Okay, so fruit is off the table. But veggies are still on. Good to know that I can still refer to you with an eggplant in chat."

I glared at him evilly after that. Neither Romeo nor Mercutio had explained to me what they meant when they used that emoji online, but I wasn't stupid and had googled it myself.

*Pervs.*

"Anyway, I am just glad she got off your back," Mercutio said with a smile.

"Me too," I said with a sigh of relief. "I suppose her mom will be happy she is dating a Capulet," I muttered. "I personally don't see the appeal in dating a Capulet. Do you?"

*Got him.*

[133]

He tilted his head, a smirk playing on his lips and a mischievous twinkle in his eyes. He was about to answer when a sudden commotion disrupted our conversation.

"Emergency, boys!" Rosaline's voice sliced through the air, her form a blinding silhouette against the bright sun as she approached us with determined strides. She grabbed my hand, her grip firm, and reached for Mercutio with the other.

*I would not get my answer today.*

"An emergency?" Mercutio quirked an eyebrow but allowed himself to be pulled to his feet.

"Come on!" Her urgency brooked no argument, and we followed her lead, half-stumbling in our haste.

"Where are we going?" I asked, trying to keep up with her long strides.

"Trust me, it's important," Rosaline insisted, dragging us forward with determination.

We rounded a corner and found ourselves outside a cozy coffee shop, its windows showing it was filled with warmth and laughter. Through the glass, I glimpsed Romeo, his golden hair catching the soft glow of fairy lights strung overhead, his smile directed at someone who wasn't one of us.

*Juliet.*

[134]

"Romeo seems fine to me," I said, confusion wrinkling my brow as I observed their easy banter, the way they leaned into each other's space like matching pieces of a puzzle.

"Too fine," Rosaline countered, her expression darkening like the clouds above. "We have to save Juliet from his charm offensive. Who knows what heartache might unfold?"

Mercutio scoffed lightly, though the humor didn't quite reach his eyes. "Let them be, Rose. They're just enjoying the dance of new love."

I snickered at his poeticism. Trust Mercutio to come up with such eloquent ways to describe love.

"New love is like a rose," Rosaline shot back, her voice sharp. "Beautiful to behold, yet hiding the pain of its prick."

"You've got that quote from someone," I muttered, but my voice was drowned out by Mercutio's louder one.

"Whose prick?"

Rosaline just frowned, and without another word, she tugged us inside, the bell above the door tinkling like a prelude to our unforeseen interruption.

"I just mean, if someone's offering," Mercutio said jokingly, his voice dwindling when neither of us replied. The clink of porcelain and murmur of voices wrapped around us. My gaze lingered on Romeo and Juliet, their laughter mingling like harmonious chords. Juliet's eyes sparkled with an innocence that tugged at something deep within me.

"Rosaline," I whispered, my voice a thread of concern as I watched her face draw tighter, her eyes narrowing ever so slightly. "Are you certain this is necessary?"

"Absolutely," she replied, her tone leaving no room for doubt, though it carried the weight of an impending storm. "He'll burn through her heart and leave only ashes."

"You got that from someone, too?" I asked.

Mercutio snorted, his fuchsia hair a stark contrast against the muted decor of the shop. He turned his focus fully on Rosaline.

"You can't be serious, right?" he teased, but even he couldn't mask the unease that flickered in his deep brown eyes.

"Dead serious," Rosaline retorted, already moving forward with a resolve that seemed to bend the very air around her. Her hand found my arm, gripping with an urgency that propelled me after her shadow.

*Why me?* Why couldn't she have dragged Mercutio along with her first?

Rosaline was strong for a girl of her age and posture. It was upsetting, really, how easily she pulled me along. I could feel Mercutio trailing behind us, his usual bravado hushed by the tension of the impending encounter. I knew we were both thinking the same. *Romeo will kill us. He will never forgive us for interrupting his date.*

As we joined the table, transforming Romeo's date into an unexpected group gathering, Romeo's expression shifted from delight to dismay. His golden brows knit together as his eyes met ours.

"Rosaline? Benvolio? Mercutio?" Romeo's voice rose above the quiet din, confusion lacing his words. "What's going on?"

"Hi, we were just passing by and thought we could join you," Rosaline said, clearly faking a smile. I couldn't help but think I admired her for the way she approached Romeo. It was clear what our intentions were… to interrupt and sabotage his date. But still, Rosaline managed to bring it all with such tact that it was hard for Romeo to send us all away. She had already sat herself down next to Juliet, without waiting for an answer or permission, and turned to her.

"Hi, my name is Rosaline." Then she faked a frown. "Wait, haven't I seen you somewhere before?"

Juliet's smile faltered, a crease forming between her brows as she glanced between us all, clearly trying to stitch together the sudden turn of events. But it was Romeo whose chagrin was most pronounced, his mouth opening and

[137]

closing without sound. *My poor, confused cousin.*

"Ah, the movie theater! Popcorn girl!" Rosaline exclaimed a bit too loudly so everyone around her could hear. She clapped her hands together in a display of joyfulness. At this point, I could no longer tell if she was still acting or if her reactions were genuine.

"So good to see you again," she concluded with the widest smile. Juliet's frown had completely dissipated at Rosaline's warm introduction, and the two girls instantly started chatting as if they were old friends.

I let my eyes wander to meet Mercutio's, both of us looking at each other for guidance. I watched him shrug, then saw how he plopped down on the chair next to Romeo. I sat down as well, with the boys to my left and the girls to my right. In between their worlds, so to speak.

"So, tell me," Mercutio started, slouching in the chair casually like this was any other day and not a romantic date he was ruining. "Where have you taken her today?"

Romeo's expression was dark and sour, his brows drawn in displeasure and his lips pursed. "Well, I have taken her for a walk across the *Ponte Pietra*. And I was going to take her to *Via Cappello* to see the Gothic balcony there."

Then he leaned closer to Mercutio and spoke quietly through gritted teeth. "But you guys have got to go. Juliet and I were going to do *stuff*."

"Juliet seems just fine to me," Mercutio retorted swiftly, inclining his head toward Juliet, who seemed to be engaged in lively conversation with Rosaline. The two girls were talking animatedly, with lots of hand gestures and bright smiles, which only upset Romeo even further. He huffed and leaned his chin on his hand, then picked up a coaster with the other hand and started to toy with it.

"Fine," he relented, and my heart did a little leap of victory. *We'd done it*. We had busted Romeo's date, and he hadn't killed us for it *yet*. In fact, Juliet seemed to truly be enjoying our company, being all smiles with Rosaline and eventually opening up to both Mercutio and me.

The conversation stumbled into a semblance of normalcy. We talked about education, hobbies, and future dreams, which only made us realize how serious a girl Juliet was. She wanted to make a career, to become a lawyer, to settle in a nice home. And as she told us this, she glanced at Romeo, flashing him a smile that said it all.

*Yeah, she definitely needed to find someone else*. I hate to admit it, but she was too good for my cousin, very much out of his league. Romeo's dreams were different. I briefly locked eyes with Mercutio, a silent understanding passing between us. He was thinking the same.

[139]

Laughter rippled across our table. Rosaline's eyes, usually so impassive, flickered with an intensity that belied her calm demeanor as she chatted with Juliet. It was a sight both rare and intriguing. Rosaline usually wasn't this lively around others, especially strangers. Then again, the girls did seem to have a lot in common. So it was no surprise that when Rosaline checked her phone and realized she had to leave, she seemed genuinely disappointed.

"Guys, I really must go," Rosaline announced, breaking the spell.

"Already?" Juliet's voice held a note of genuine disappointment, the subtlest tremble beneath the surface.

"Unfortunately, yes." Rosaline glanced at her phone, the screen a beacon summoning her away from us. She rose gracefully, flashing us a smile.

Juliet parted her lips to say something, but then Rosaline's phone chimed, and she cursed audibly. "That'll be Livia asking me where I am. She's covering for me. I really need to be off. Bye!"

And with that, she was gone. I watched Juliet closely as her smile seemed to fall, and her fingers twitched. *Interesting*. My gaze met Juliet's.

"You okay?" I ventured, my voice barely

[140]

more than a whisper.

She nodded, a silent affirmation that was as much for herself as it was for me. "Yeah, just... didn't expect things to go this way."

"Me neither," Romeo grumbled as he got up from his chair, "I think we should go as well. Let me get the bill."

We watched him go, Mercutio turning around to observe our friend as he walked up to the counter, card in hand. At least he was going to pay for his date. I wryly remembered the many times he hadn't bothered to do so. The last time I recalled was at the movie theater, where he had hoped to woo Rosaline. *And met Juliet.* How quickly his attention had shifted from one girl to the next.

"Life is rarely as we expect," I murmured. "But sometimes, the unexpected moments linger the longest."

"That sounds beautiful," Juliet mused softly, her lips curving into a wistful smile.

A thought hit me. Juliet had a click with Rosaline; anyone with eyes could see that. I heavily suspected she was upset that they couldn't exchange numbers before Rosaline left. Perhaps I could mediate? Plus, it could be a good thing if she had my number, just in case Romeo did something stupid and she needed someone to talk to.

*In case he broke her heart.*

[141]

"Would you—um, would you maybe want to exchange numbers?"

"Sure," she said, her smile brightening. "I liked talking to you. It's nice to get to know Romeo's friends."

I fumbled for my phone.

"What's this, Benvolio?" Mercutio's voice sliced through the moment as his attention shifted to us, his tone teasing yet sharp enough to draw blood. "Be careful Romeo doesn't spot you two swapping numbers, or he might get jealous."

Why did he sound so... *harsh?* Bitter?

I felt my cheeks grow warm, and I turned to him with a scowl. "It's called being friendly, Merc. You know, like a good Montague."

"Uh-huh." Mercutio cocked an eyebrow, his fuchsia hair catching the light as he leaned back, a Cheshire Cat basking in the glow of mischief. "I know all about the friendliness of the Montagues."

His eyes drifted back to Romeo while he wiggled his eyebrows, insinuating that by 'friendliness,' he meant Romeo's flirting behavior, and I sputtered.

*The horror.* How dare he compare me to Romeo and his hopeless romantic heart. *Again.* I wanted to protest, but Mercutio was already distracted. I saw concern etched on his features and the slight dip of his brow as he frowned while his eyes rested on my cousin. I followed his gaze.

His worries about Romeo witnessing our number exchange seemed to have been unnecessary. For there he was, my cousin. His attention was captured entirely by a waitress who stood giggling at his side, his eyes never leaving her. I watched as she brushed a strand of pale hair behind her ear, her eyes glittering with mirth. A gaze I had seen too often.

She was falling for his charm.

So he had done it again. He'd captured a new girl's interest. And the worst thing was, I could tell that the feeling was mutual. Romeo had a new infatuation coming on.

*Well, shit.*

They were talking, hands moving in low gestures, soft chuckles reaching my ears as they smiled brightly, their eyes never leaving each other. I snapped my gaze back to Juliet to see that she was scrolling on her phone and prayed she hadn't noticed yet.

A gentle smile curled Juliet's lips while she raised her phone to show me a picture of Romeo and her together, his arm wrapped around her waist as they stood on the most romantic bridge Verona had to offer.

"He said there isn't any other girl for him but me," she whispered, her voice so soft I could barely hear her over the buzz of voices and

[143]

cutlery clinking. "Said he can't live without me," she sighed, and a dreamy look appeared in her gaze. "No one has ever said that to me before."

I bet they hadn't. They probably never had the chance to do so. By the sound of it, Juliet had been living a rather sheltered life, always busy with schoolwork and getting good grades because she wanted to make it in the world. She never had the time to date silly boys. How Romeo had managed to persuade her to go out with him was beyond me.

Juliet leaned a little closer, the pictures on her phone sliding by, one by one, showing the two of them together. Laughing. Smiling. Noses touching.

At that exact moment, Romeo and the waitress laughed together, a private joke blossoming between them.

"I think Romeo is done paying," I heard Mercutio's voice, a little sharper edge to it than usual. He, too, had watched them with distaste.

We had to admit that Rosaline had been right. At first, I had thought she had wanted to interrupt Romeo's date out of jealousy. That somehow, she had changed her mind about him. They say *you don't know what you have until you've lost it*, and I thought this could be such a case. I see now that I was wrong. She hadn't acted out of spite or jealousy.

She'd truly been concerned.

Juliet was a nice girl and too good to be with someone like my cousin Romeo, who was still finding himself. They didn't want the same things, as our conversation had made painfully clear. Romeo was Romeo. He could not help it, his heart was easily swayed. I sometimes wondered if he was looking in the right direction.

But that didn't mean we, his friends, shouldn't protect the girls he fell helplessly in love with. We had rescued some of them from his affection before.

It seemed like Juliet was the next one we had to save.

# *Eight*

*"W*hat did you think of the new guy?" the message in the chat said.

"*Kinda cute.*" Mercutio's reply was adorned with pink hearts. I had to stifle a chuckle.

"*What kind of name is Paris, anyway?*" another Montague friend replied, their message oozing annoyance. "*Who names their kid after a city?*"

"*It's a fashionable name.*" Another friend.

"*Cute,*" Mercutio piped in again.

I rolled my eyes and slid my phone back into my pocket, trying to ignore the fact that Mercutio had just called this Paris guy cute.

Time to get back to work.

The scent of new leather filled my nostrils as I methodically stacked boxes of shoes, one atop the other, creating a makeshift fortress around me.

My thoughts went to Romeo and Juliet. The absence of Romeo's presence in the chat was noticeable. Romeo was always like this, either very much present and lamenting about a love he couldn't get, or completely ignoring us whenever he got a girl to date him. *Those periods of silence never lasted long, though.*

I was lost in thought when the bell above

the door jangled with force.

"Hello, Benvolio," Livia's voice sliced through the air, each syllable dripping with disdain. I suppose she was still angry with me then…

She stood there, framed by the doorway, her bleached hair with defiant red streaks almost ablaze in the sunlight streaming in from outside. I straightened up, placing the last box on the pile.

"Livia," I said evenly, brushing dust off my hands, "How good to see you."

And I meant it. Even though I felt somewhat nervous about being in her presence again, on my own, with no one here except for Laurence to save me. And let's be honest, Laurence wasn't known for being very observant. Plus, he didn't know Livia had wanted to date me and was now angry with me. *Such a mess I was in, ugh.* I doubted Laurence would come to my rescue.

But I still considered Livia a friend, even if I wanted to avoid her. They say *'hell hath no fury like a woman scorned'*, and it was obvious that she was still seething even after weeks. I had to remind myself I hadn't done anything intentionally to get her in this state.

"Good to see me?" she spat, storming closer. Her eyes were two dark storms, and her presence charged the space between us with static. "You didn't bother replying to me for weeks, you're avoiding me," she said accusingly, pointing at me.

"And don't think I didn't know about you and my sister hanging out! I know that Rosaline was covering for you." She let out an agitated sigh and I listened in silence.

"I know how you two met up with the others without asking me to come along. And now you just smile and pretend that everything is normal between us?"

What could I say to that? She clearly had misinterpreted things here. I had just been friendly with her, considering her one of my best friends and nothing more. Was that a crime?

"Anyway," she said, tossing her head back with a haughty air, "I figured that if you don't come to me, then I could just come to you."

"So you're not here to buy shoes?" I asked, already knowing the answer. I watched Livia as she tilted her head to sneer down at me, and shyly scratched my head as I smiled back at her. "Never mind," I whispered.

She frowned and folded her arms in front of her chest. "My sister's been suspiciously quiet. But I caught her sneaking off a few times. Saw her walking into Montague territory," she eyed me suspiciously. "Care to tell me what she's been up to?"

Was that the reason she had cornered me here at my job? I let my shoulders sag and came to stand opposite her, leaning carefully against one of the shoe racks.

"She's been concerned about Romeo's newest conquest," I admitted, earning a scoff from Livia's lips.

"You want me to believe she's been visiting your part of the city just to keep Romeo from dating someone else?" Livia let out a dry laugh because this sounded incredibly atypical for Rosaline. I knew it was hard to believe, but it was the sad truth.

"Come on, Benvolio, you can do better than that," she then challenged me, a haughty look slipped on her features, her lips curled into a smirk. "Don't tell me you *dumped* me because you wanted to date my sister."

I froze. Where on earth did she get that idea from? Staring at her, with my lips parted and eyes wide, I could tell that she was taking delight in studying my shocked expression. She stood a little taller now, as if she'd just achieved some form of victory, and tapped her fingers against her own arm.

"Well, well, would you look at that? Here you are, trying to be such a gentleman when in reality, you are as much of a player as your cousin. But I am onto you." She jotted a finger accusingly at my chest. "Both of you. Rosaline

[149]

can't hide the truth forever."

Did she really think her own sister had been sneaking out of the house just to see me? I wasn't sure if I should take it as a compliment or an insult. And did she just compare me to Romeo? What was up with people doing that lately? I hadn't been flirting with anyone. *Not on purpose anyway.*

"We're," I stammered, "We're not—"

A searing heat crept up my neck, the unfairness of her accusation igniting a fire within, and yet my mouth was too numb to utter a word. I could feel the tremor in my hands, tucked out of sight behind my back.

Livia's gaze bore into me with an intensity that made my insides churn. She stood with one hip cocked, her eyes narrowed. "Anyway, it doesn't matter. I moved on." Though it didn't really sound like she had. But I silently prayed she would have found a nice new boy to focus on. The sooner she forgot about her crush on me, the better.

"Rosaline is really missing out," she continued, unaware of the thoughts racing through my head. "Our parents wanted her to date this *wonderful* young man. A Capulet, wealthy, good-looking. Can't believe she turned him down just to be with you."

I wondered how much more Livia had misinterpreted. To first think that we were an item, and to now assume that I had started dating her sister instead. It was weird. I could tell her that Rosaline hadn't turned down a date with *a fine Capulet man*—if they even existed—to be with me, but it was clear that Livia was on a roll and didn't wish to be interrupted, so I waited for her to be done with her rant.

"Emilio Capulet," she pronounced the name like a spell meant to conjure envy. "I'm sure you've heard of him."

I had. A recent memory of reading a post written by his hand emerged. He was one of Tybalt's friends.

*Someone who knew about him and Mercutio.*

I quickly turned away, only realizing a little too late that the action must have given Livia the impression that her words stung me. They did, just not in the way she had intended them to.

"Anyway, he is hot. I didn't understand why Rosaline wouldn't want him. I mean, I figured it out now, obviously," *not so obviously*, I thought, pressing my lips into a thin line because oh boy, *she was so wrong.*

"But Emilio has got it all. Such a gentleman," the unspoken *'unlike you'* lingered in the air, emphasized by the look she threw at me straight after. She quirked a brow and studied me, waiting for a reaction. But I remained calm, merely frowned at her as I

[151]

leaned back against the rack filled with shoes.

So, Livia tried to make me feel jealous by telling me she was dating another boy. If anything, I felt relieved. And I figured I might as well honestly tell her that.

"Emilio is lucky," I said.

"Indeed, he is," Livia replied, her gaze flickering with triumph. But beneath the bravado, I could see something else that I couldn't quite pinpoint.

"I am happy you found someone nice," *so you can forget about me.* "You deserve someone who takes care of you."

Livia frowned, "Now you're just saying that to make me feel better," she grumbled, gritting her teeth. But I shook my head almost instantly, being as honest as I could be with her.

"It's true. You're my friend, Livia. And I am sorry I upset you or gave you the wrong idea about us," I said earnestly. "But as a friend, I want what is best for you, and that is a man who can love you fully, someone who can treat you right. If Emilio is that man, then I am happy for you."

And I meant it. I shifted slightly, putting my weight on my other leg. My voice remained soft. "And if he turns out to be not so nice after all, well, then you can always come to me and Romeo and Mercutio. We can always hide behind the Montague and Capulet feud thing,

[152]

you know?"

Her stormy facade wavered, confusion flashing across her features. She opened her mouth, likely to throw another accusation, but then she changed her mind. Her shoulders sagged a little, her posture became less grand.

"Thank you?" she whispered, visibly and audibly uncertain how to react to my words. I wasn't bothered by her confusion. I merely shrugged and smiled at her.

"And you know, Rosaline isn't interested in dating anyone, so I think that must be why she turned Emilio down. He sounds like a nice man, but Rosaline is peculiar like that. I don't know if she will ever find someone she is interested in," I furrowed my brows while I raked my brain for a memory of Rosaline ever looking at someone with interest like that. I couldn't quite tell if a moment like that had ever occurred. Except perhaps recently, with Juliet. But perhaps I was reading too much into it.

"So you're still single?" Livia carefully asked, her voice small and light and no longer accusing.

"I'm not taken," I said, but a tug at the strings of my heart made me wonder if that was true. Why did my heart ache so badly whenever I spoke of love?

Something swirled inside my chest again like it had been doing more often lately, and I instantly braced myself for the oncoming cough that was about to follow. *Not again,* I groaned inwardly, willing the nauseousness to go away and the tickle in my throat to quiet.

"You swear you're not dating Rosaline?" Livia asked me, still mistrusting me a little.

I flashed her what I hoped was a comforting smile. "I swear. Livia, you mean a lot to me. Why would I lie to you?"

She fell silent, a pout on her lips while her dark eyes darted to the floor. "Oh."

*Yes, oh,* I thought. I raised a hand gently, gesturing for her to wait. I still had something I wanted to give to her, and now that she was finally calming down, I thought it might be the right time.

I turned, taking measured steps toward the counter where a small, neatly wrapped package lay hidden from view. Luckily, the feeling inside my chest subsided a little, the tickle fading just enough to allow me to breathe properly again.

"Before you go," I began, my voice soft but firm, "there's something I want you to have." I reached for the gift, feeling its weight in my hands.

Returning to her, I extended the present. "For you, Livia. I saw these and thought of you. I know how much you love drawing."

She hesitated, giving me a look that said

she was both curious and not completely trusting me, but then carefully unwrapped the paper. The designer digital drawing pens revealed themselves, their sleek form mimicking the elegance of quills from another era. I watched as recognition dawned on her.

"Ben... these are..." Livia's voice trailed off, and I could see the shift in her demeanor. The earlier heat of her anger cooled into something softer, regretful. "I... I don't know what to say. This is too much. I was so mad at you, and you... You're still being kind to me."

"Don't worry, I still see you as a friend. And friends can give each other gifts, right?" I replied, the ghost of a smile playing on my lips.

Her gaze dropped to the pens she now cradled in her hands. "You always know how to make someone feel special. You're," here she groaned, a painful sound that erupted from her lips. "I've been such a fool."

Livia looked up, her bleached hair with red strands framing her face in stark contrast to the vulnerability that now played across her features. "I'm sorry, Ben. For earlier... I shouldn't have said those things. I was mad, and I tried," her voice broke off, and she shook her head, "I tried to make you feel bad."

"Hey," I started gently. "It's okay, Livia."

She hesitated, then inhaled sharply. "No, it's not okay. I've not been a good friend. You've

[155]

always been kind to me," she hesitated. "A thousand times kinder than Emilio could ever be."

*Emilio.* I silently wondered if I could talk to him privately one day and ask him about Mercutio and Tybalt. My thoughts started drifting off, but Livia was still talking, stammering.

A flush crept onto Livia's cheeks, and she bit her lip, almost shyly. "More handsome, too," she added in a hushed tone before looking up at me with eyes full of confession.

*Oh no.* That hadn't been the reaction I had hoped for. *Great, Benvolio, you have done it again,* I thought to myself, feeling embarrassed by Livia's reaction. Was I unintentionally screwing things up again just by being kind?

"It's just a gift," I murmured, knowing that she didn't hear as her words already drifted over mine.

"I think I'm in love with you, Benvolio."

*Not again.* A sigh escaped me. I brought my hand up to my forehead and squeezed my eyes shut. Her declaration, earnest and raw, hung heavy in the air, but it was a song meant for a different listener's heart.

I didn't love her.

"Livia," I said, the kindness I felt for her threading through each syllable, "you are wonderful, truly, but your heart isn't for me. It

[156]

beats a rhythm meant for another."

*Like how mine is beating for another,* the thought rose involuntarily, and the shimmering image of Mercutio shortly appeared before my eyes. *But Mercutio doesn't love me,* I thought dejectedly. He was dating Tybalt. *Probably.*

I shouldn't wish for something that wasn't mine to have. It was unfair for both of us.

Livia's eyes searched mine, seeking a foothold in a landslide of rejection. She nodded, a silent crestfallen agreement.

"Okay," she whispered, her voice a fractured echo of her earlier defiance. She clutched the pens tightly. "I'll try to understand." With a sad shrug, she whispered, "Just friends."

"Just friends," I confirmed, hoping that after this, she would finally let it rest. As I watched her step away, her image shimmered and turned into Mercutio.

*Just friends*, the words echoed inside my head, and I suddenly felt them again; petals clawing their way up my throat.

His laughter, his wildness. Everything about him was a stark contrast to the calm I presented to the world. All these things I could not have. Only see from the sidelines. *As a friend.*

Livia paused at the door, shimmering back to herself. She cast back a smile that was more wound than joy.

[157]

"I'll see you around then?" she asked, hesitating.

All I managed was a nod, but it was enough. She flashed me another sad smile, and I watched as she reached for the door, her hand trembling.

The petals in my throat ached, but I had to keep them down. I had to keep up the pretense that all was well.

The door's soft chime signaled her departure. A few racks behind me, I heard Laurence let out a deep sigh. He'd probably been eavesdropping. *Shit,* I had so much to explain to him. I didn't even know where to start.

Just then, a tightness clenched my throat, and it became too much to hide. I swallowed hard, once, twice, but the uprising within was relentless.

I caught a glimpse of Livia's retreating form through the glass, her hand lifting in a pained farewell, and was grateful that she wouldn't have to be here to see this and worry over me.

A strangled gasp ripped from my lips. Petals, soft and crimson, spilled over my tongue, fluttering to land disgracefully upon the polished leather of a new shoe that was in front of me on the counter.

They lay there, stark against the dark surface, vivid and bright, *and undeniably there.*

[158]

Not just one but a small cascade of them. My symptoms were becoming worse, and still, I tried to pretend I wasn't suffering from anything. No disease. No nothing.

I was fine. Peachy.

"Are you all right, Benvolio?" Laurence's voice, laced with concern, broke through my wall of solitude.

I turned, hastily brushing at the tears that threatened to betray me further, and faced him with a feigned calm I was far from feeling.

"Yes, just... allergies." The excuse felt feeble even to my own ears, but Laurence seemed to consider it with only a slight wrinkle of his brow.

"Where did these come from?" He gestured to the petals that I had no chance to hide. His frown deepened, a crease of confusion etching between his concerned eyes. *Was he studying them?*

"Ah, must've been blown in by the wind," I managed, my voice uneven. I saw Laurence's eyes dart around the room, searching for a possible source. He nodded slowly, though I could tell he wasn't entirely convinced.

"Well, best get rid of them," he said, eyeing the shoe and the petals that covered it.

"Of course," I murmured, bending to obey. My fingers trembled as they gathered the delicate petals that had been inside me mere

[159]

moments ago. I realized I should probably go and consult a doctor, and made a mental note to go make an appointment during my break. *Was I growing a tree inside of me?* Had that ever happened to anyone before? That was physically and biologically impossible, right?

As I let the last petals float from my palm into the nearest trash can, a digital chirp broke the silence. I turned to glance at Laurence, but he had moved further into the store and pretended he was busy doing something. I then dusted off my hands before reaching into the back pocket of my jeans.

The screen of my phone glowed with Mercutio's name, his words appearing like the prelude to yet another storm.

*"Romeo's done it again,"* read the message.

I sighed, my thumb hovering over the keys as I contemplated how to approach this latest drama. Before I could type a response, another message popped up, this time from Romeo himself.

*"I know Mercutio has sent you a message, and I swear it's okay. I was just hanging out with Suzy,"* he wrote, and I frowned. Who was Suzy?

And so I typed my reply. *"Who's Suzy?"*

*"Uh, don't you know?"* The reply was instant. I saw the dotted lines as Romeo typed, then felt my phone buzz when a new message came in. At least he was no longer ignoring us.

*"The waitress."*

"The waitress?" I murmured, furrowing my brow. The name flitted through my memory like a leaf caught in the wind. I never heard it before. When I tried to think of any waitresses we'd seen recently, my thoughts finally landed on the image of a girl with a warm smile, coffee pot in hand, the two of them whispering and smiling while we were chatting with Juliet.

*Oh, that waitress.*

Was he serious?

*"Ah, yes. Of course,"* I replied, though I had scarcely taken note of her at the time. "Romeo, be sensible for a moment," I grumbled, more to myself than to anyone else. *"You mean the waitress who served us during that date you had with Juliet?"*

*"That date you crashed,"* came Romeo's instant reply.

I rolled my eyes and sighed. That was a yes, then.

*"I caught them,"* Mercutio buzzed in between. *"But haven't told Juliet yet. Do you think we need to tell her?"* The emojis he sent along indicated he was anticipating drama and already loving it. Perhaps this was yet another reason why he had become friends with Romeo. He loved to be the gossip girl, and Romeo provided gossip aplenty with his love life problems.

*"Seems I've got a thing for women who serve*

*me drinks,"* Romeo quipped, distracting me from Mercutio's messages, and I could almost hear his laughter ringing through the text.

My jaw tightened imperceptibly, a reaction I concealed even from myself. Romeo's heart was such a curious thing. A heart that leaped from Juliet to Suzy as easily as one might change shoes. A good metaphor, I know.

Rosaline had been right. Not that there had been any doubt, but still... I had hoped that this time it would have been different, that Romeo would have grown up a bit and would have been serious about his relationships for once. Juliet was. She had thought about her future and had goals she wanted to achieve. What did Romeo want in life?

Perhaps he should try and date someone completely different for once. Perhaps he would finally discover what he truly wanted.

I decided to leave Romeo be, swapped back to Mercutio, and sent a message that was supposed to calm him down. It worked, for not much later, I received an array of different colored hearts that made me chuckle.

*"You trying to imitate the rainbow?"* I replied, earning me a capitalized *'YES'* and some more hearts in all the colors my phone could handle.

Tucking the phone into my pocket with a chuckle and an amused shake of the head, I turned back to the day's tasks. I spared one last glance at the trash can, thinking of the petals in there. But then I shrugged and turned back as the bell chimed to signal the arrival of a customer.

# Nine

The afternoon sun carved shadows on the pavement as I made my way through the crowded streets, the chatter of the city a dull hum in my ears. Romeo was talking to us again, which was a good thing. Mercutio seemed relieved about it, though he was still worried whether or not we should tell Juliet. I'd shared that Livia finally got the cue and understood that I wasn't interested, a message which Mercutio answered with a 'THANK GOD'. The capitalized words kept flashing in my mind and made me wear a smile for the remainder of the day.

Even now, as I was on my way home, my mind was elsewhere, lost in thoughts of fuchsia hair and laughter that rang like bells. I didn't notice someone had come to block my way until a shadow fell over me.

"Montague."

The voice was sharp enough to slice through my reverie, pulling me back to the here and now. Tybalt Capulet stood before me, his long black curls framing a face that held the kind of beauty found in daggers, sleek, dangerous, and not to be trifled with.

The last person I wanted to see. Ever. Unbidden images of Mercutio appeared, his

[164]

back arched, Tybalt hunched over him.

*Why? Why had he chosen the tall Capulet and kept it a secret from us all?*

"Tybalt," I replied, my tone measured, betraying none of the sudden unease that gripped me. I could have said '*Capulet*', but I didn't want to play whatever game he had in mind. We knew each other's names. And I knew that whatever he was to say next wasn't going to be nice.

Our eyes locked, and time stretched thin between us. His gaze, intense and unyielding, bore into me like a warning.

"Walk with me," he commanded more than requested, and I felt the gravity of what this meant. The air was charged with tension thick enough to choke on.

"Mercutio," Tybalt began, the name falling from his lips with a hint of tenderness, "what is he to you?"

I swallowed hard, forcing casualness into my voice. "He's a friend, nothing more." The lie tasted bitter. *Mercutio was everything*.

"Friend," he scoffed, his probing eyes searching mine for the truth I dared not reveal. "You're always there, shadowing him like some lovesick—"

*Now, wait a minute. What was this all about?*

"Tybalt," I interrupted, hoping to steer

away from dangerous territory. "What business is it of yours?"

He stopped abruptly, causing me to halt mid-step. His face hovered close, and I could smell the Eau de Cologne that clung to him like an invisible armor. There was something else beneath it, something raw and perhaps a little desperate.

"Because," he said, each word laden with an intensity that set my heart racing, "I know what it's like to want something you shouldn't."

His confession hung in the air, and I suddenly understood. The hostility, the glances. He saw too much of himself in me, saw the concealed yearning mirrored in my eyes.

"Tybalt," I breathed out, the name feeling strange on my tongue, "I—"

For the first time, I couldn't deny it to myself. I wasn't just afraid that Tybalt would win his heart and that Mercutio would forget me. *I wanted Mercutio.* I was jealous of what he and Tybalt had done. The kiss they had shared.

"Save it, Montague," he cut me off. Tybalt's fingers dug into the fabric of my collar, pulling me close enough that I could smell the cologne clinging to his skin, a sharp contrast to the acrid scent of fear seeping from my pores. His breath was hot against my cheek, each word punctuated by a clenching of his jaw, a tightening of his grip.

[166]

"You're a pretty boy, Benvolio, so I'll give you a warning. I don't want you anywhere near him, or you won't be so pretty after. Got it?" His hot breath ghosted my skin, and his warm body was pressed uncomfortably close to mine. I suddenly understood how Mercutio had wanted to be touched by him when this was how it felt.

A bitter chuckle escaped Tybalt's lips before they brushed past my jaw. "Friends, my ass," he muttered, and I felt the scrape of his teeth with every word he spoke. "I won't let you ruin this."

And I wondered what 'this' was. *What was I ruining? Their secret relationship?*

Strong, calloused fingers brushed past my skin, squeezing my jaw while he leaned in a little closer. And then he pushed himself away, the distance between us growing until I felt I could breathe again.

"Consider this your only warning," his voice rasped. I watched him turn on his heel, taking a moment to pause as he debated whether or not to turn to me and say something more. But then he seemed to make up his mind and straightened his spine before he walked away, a storm contained within the lines of his retreating form. As he disappeared into the crowd, I was left standing alone, with a racing heart and the echo of his threat lingering in my mind.

A petal, the color of heartache, tumbled from my lips to the pavement. The pink stood out against the drab concrete. The sight of it sent a shiver down my spine as I tried to wrap my mind around Tybalt's earlier words and what they implied. My heart was a frightened bird in my chest, its wings fluttering wildly against the cage of my ribs. My pulse thrummed in my ears, a cacophony that drowned out the noise of the street.

I ran a trembling hand through my short curls, trying to anchor myself to the present, to dispel the heavy fog of uncertainty that clouded my mind.

Mercutio—bright, vibrant Mercutio—was *more* than just a friend. He was the enigma that kept me awake at night, the laughter that coaxed smiles from my reluctant lips, the riddle I yearned to solve. I couldn't stay away from him; it simply wasn't an option, despite the danger in Tybalt's words.

A sharp pain cleaved through my chest, halting my flight. Doubling over, I grasped at the fabric of my shirt, my fingers clenching as if they could squeeze out the anguish that gripped me. The air in my lungs felt like shards of glass; every attempt to breathe was a battle. Then, the coughing started, a violent, relentless torrent that shook my frame.

My knees buckled as the first petal

[168]

fluttered to the ground, a pale pink whisper against the harsh concrete. More followed, a cascade of them, torn from the depths of my chest by each convulsive hack. They littered the pavement, fragrant and soft. So beautiful, it was hard to think they came from me, or that I indeed was choking on them. I stared at them as they kept coming forth, coloring the street pink.

I realized I had forgotten to call the doctor to make an appointment today. It had been too busy with customers. It could wait a little longer, I told myself.

*There's nothing wrong with me. This would pass.*

Gritting my teeth, I forced myself upright, my hands covering my mouth in a futile attempt to stem the flow of petals. They spilled through the gaps between my fingers, relentless in their escape. Each one felt like a piece of my soul, torn away and left to wither on the ground.

I ignored the stares of people passing by as I stumbled forward, a trail of petals in my wake.

I wouldn't avoid Mercutio. I wouldn't abandon him as a friend. No matter what threats Tybalt would throw at me.

I wouldn't stay away from Mercutio.

# Ten

A good meal can make you forget the troubles of the day. And although I was far from being a chef, my cooking skills were pretty decent. The scent of my solitary dinner still lingered in the air, a mix of roasted garlic and thyme that clung to the corners of the dimly lit room.

It was several weeks after my run-in with Tybalt, and I hadn't listened to his threat. I still met up with Mercutio. Romeo was still fooling around with Juliet *and* Suzy. And I still hadn't called the doctor to make an appointment.

There had been a few petals, but not as many as after I had run into Tybalt. I kept forgetting—or rather kept postponing—having myself checked. My days were busy enough, and I enjoyed my evenings spent with friends. Or, like tonight, by myself. Have a bit of rest after a hard day's work.

I hadn't bothered with the lights; the evening's soft glow was enough to keep the shadows at bay, offering a semblance of peace. The window was cracked open just enough for the evening breeze to carry in the distant hum of city traffic, blending with the occasional rustle of leaves from the old oak tree outside.

I was reclining on the chair, phone in hand, my legs stretched out and crossed at the ankles, just enjoying the peace and quiet, when a scraping, shuffling noise against the side of the building was heard. Curiosity piqued, I rose. It was only when I approached the window that a shadowy figure became visible behind it. *Like the shadow of a man.*

My breath caught in my throat, and I felt my heart beat high in my chest. This was impossible. I heard the knocks next. Not made by a creature or by twigs. But real, human knocks.

While I was on the third floor.

*This was insane.*

I took a step closer to see the familiar face of my cousin appear, smiling sheepishly at me from behind the glass.

"Can you open this?" he asked, his voice more of a whine that betrayed his panic. "Quickly, please."

"Romeo?" I whispered, incredulity lacing my tone as I yanked the window wide open. There he was, dangling from the sill, his blond hair disheveled, his shirt clinging to his defined abs from exertion or fear, I couldn't tell which.

*How did he get up here,* I wondered as I stared at him in awe. This was a feat I could have expected from Mercutio, who was skilled at parkour, but from *Romeo*?

"Ben, help me up," he gasped, and I obliged, pulling him into the safety of my room.

[171]

Once inside, he collapsed onto the floor, panting heavily, his forehead glistening with sweat. The adrenaline from his climb still seemed to course through his veins, making him jittery, his eyes darting around the room.

"Romeo, what on earth are you doing?" I demanded, pressing my back against the cool glass of the now-closed window, trying to steady my own racing pulse. Whatever was going on, he had a lot of explaining to do.

Romeo struggled to find his breath, his hands shaking as he slowly pushed himself up until he was on his knees, looking up at me. "It's... It's Juliet," he finally managed to utter, his voice carrying the weight of impending doom.

"Slow down. What about Juliet?" I insisted, kneeling beside him to meet his gaze.

"Caught me... she caught me, Benvolio," he stammered, his flushed face a portrait of guilt and desperation.

"Caught you? Caught you doing what, Romeo?" My question hung between us, although we both knew at this point what Romeo was going to say.

"With another girl..." Suzy, probably. Though I wasn't a hundred percent sure. Romeo's puppy-eyed look could have fooled anyone, except me. I had known my cousin since we were toddlers and had spent so much time with him that I had become immune to his charm. Whatever had happened must have been pretty bad if my cousin had seen no alternative but to climb up to my window.

"Why, Romeo? Why did you do it again?" I let out a long breath, the sound less of surprise and more of a desolate echo of disappointment. He finally had been in with a real chance. He had found a girl he had fallen in love with, and who, and this is another crucial part of it, *was in love with him*. Hadn't we told him to stop seeing Suzy if he truly was so serious about Juliet?

Romeo's indignation was immediate, his hands thrown up in defense as he scrambled to his feet. "How do you mean 'again'?" he retorted, as if he had not tread this treacherous ground before.

"Romeo," I began, my tone steady despite the storm that raged within me. "You fall in love as easily as leaves from trees in autumn. Each time, you are convinced she is the one. Your true love."

He paced before me, a caged animal trapped by his own desires.

"But the feelings inside my heart, Benvolio... they're *so strong*. How can they be anything but true?" His voice trembled with passion, his eyes alight with an inner fire that refused to be quenched.

"Feelings," I mused, "they can change,

Romeo. And there's nothing wrong with that. It is okay to feel strongly about someone. But you should also consider *their* feelings. Especially when you feel strongly about someone."

I placed my hand on the windowsill, leaning in until I stood comfortably. This could take a while.

"Juliet..." Romeo muttered, pain etching lines into his youthful face. "She is the one for me. I am certain this time."

Certain? Like last time, when he was sure Rosaline was the one. Rosaline, who had told him to get lost more than once. Or the time before that. Nicole? *Wasn't he going to marry her?* And the girl before her. Didn't he want to end his life after just a week of dating because he couldn't live without her?

"So certain that you have been seeing another at the same time?" I retorted.

Romeo frowned. "Suzy is just a friend."

When would he learn?

Skeptically, I raised a brow and gave him a look I hoped would say it all.

"Mock me all you will," Romeo said, and I knew my look had worked. His eyes were earnest, his expression grave. He was serious then. Serious about having feelings, but not serious about where his relationship with Juliet could go.

Because I saw a road with a dead-end,

[174]

just like Mercutio and Rosaline had seen. Yet Romeo ignored all the signs. He steered his car into this dead-end lane and shifted gears to full speed.

*Great.*

"Juliet is the one for me, Benvolio," he said with confidence.

"And yet, she saw you with another girl?" I asked, still skeptical. "How did that happen?"

Romeo's cheeks flushed, and I could tell by the way he moved his lips in a silent murmur that he was trying to think of how to talk his way out of this one. "She's just a friend."

I stood there, my heart a dull throb in my chest, the room suddenly feeling far too small for the magnitude of Romeo's folly.

"Okay, so she is just a friend, you say," I started. *How to keep calm when talking to him like this?* I pinched my brow and had a deep think. "So Juliet saw you with... another girl? Suzy, I take it?" I asked, my voice a low murmur against the growing unease that unfurled within me.

"Yes," Romeo exhaled sharply, his gaze shifting to somewhere past my shoulder, "she saw me with Suzy."

"Suzy," I echoed, more a question than a statement, hoping against hope that the situation was not as dire as it seemed. "But you were just talking to Suzy, right?"

[175]

The words fell flat, even to my own ears, as Romeo's face betrayed the truth before his lips could form the confession. Why did I even hold hope that it had just been the two of them talking? I knew it was in vain, and Romeo's expression said it all.

"Talking, yes," he stammered, his eyes darting away, "and... I might have—"

I watched as Romeo bit his lip, too embarrassed to continue any further. *Not good*, my mind provided me.

"Romeo!" My frustration erupted. "You might have done what?"

With reluctance etched into every feature, Romeo whispered, "I might have held Suzy in my arms when Juliet walked in on us."

"Gods above," I muttered, disbelief lacing each word. "You can't be serious."

A pause stretched between us, taut like the string of a bow, ready to snap at the slightest provocation.

"And I think... Juliet might've seen us kiss," Romeo added, his voice barely a breath.

"Seen you..." My thoughts spiraled. *Seriously*. For someone claiming that Juliet was the one for him, he was behaving pretty stupidly. "And you understand why she'd be angry about that, right?"

"Angry," Romeo murmured, looking as if he wanted to snatch the words back from the air where they hung, heavy with implication.

"Of course she's angry, Romeo," I sighed. Why did he keep doing things like this?

"How would you feel if you saw the love of your life kiss and cuddle with someone else?"

*I'd be devastated,* I thought, remembering the feeling all too well. But I had to shake those memories of that dark night away.

Romeo hardly needed a moment to answer. "I'd be livid. How could she do such a thing to me?"

"Ah," I cried out, my hand flying up in the air to point at the ceiling. "Double standards, Romeo." He blinked at me as if he didn't understand what I meant by that, but I let him be.

"So you do know how it feels. You do understand." I grinned at him, glad to have achieved this little victory. Despite having known Romeo all my life, I still didn't understand how things worked inside his head.

Romeo shifted and brought his right hand up to rest on his left lower arm while he worried his lip, a clear signal that there was more to come. *Oh, heck, no.*

"Juliet wasn't even angry," he said, his voice a ragged thing, torn at the edges. "She just looked... broken."

I nodded slowly, my heart aching for her. "Broken is the right word," I said, once more remembering Mercutio pinned underneath Tybalt. That was exactly how I had felt that night.

"You might have shattered something precious inside her, Romeo," I said, swallowing the heavy memory away. "Can't you see that?"

As if to give my words more light, I walked over to one of the lamps in the corner of the room and switched it on before I leaned against the small couch I had standing there. We were suddenly bathed in a yellow glow that made everything seem warmer. Romeo's pale hair nearly seemed gold like this. Mine, too, probably.

I watched as Romeo's expression turned into a frown. He paced across the hardwood floor, his footsteps creating a rhythm my downstairs neighbors would be bound to hear.

"It wasn't supposed to be like this," he said before his dark eyes settled on me. I understood why women liked him. He had an intense gaze that sent shivers down your spine, with an angelic face and a hint of darkness. His eyes revealed a love that was never fully fulfilled. I wondered why he fell in love easily but never found his match.

As I stood pondering Romeo and his feelings, he shifted and grew quiet.

"If you and the others hadn't crashed our date, none of this would have happened,"

[178]

Romeo lamented, making my jaw drop because… *was he serious right now?* How had our joining them at the table for a drink resulted in Romeo cheating on Juliet?

"Juliet has been different since that day," Romeo continued as if he had read my mind. "She dodges my kisses, turns away from my touch." He ran a hand through his hair, a gesture of frustration and longing tangled together in the golden strands.

"Can it just be she doesn't want to take things further yet?" I asked carefully, and secretly admired Juliet for having resisted Romeo's advances. Perhaps she wasn't as naïve as I thought her to be. "She might just want you to slow down a bit. It isn't as if the world ends tomorrow, you know."

"Every time," he murmured, defeat etched into the curve of his mouth, the set of his jaw. He came to stand opposite me, frowning as his eyes sought mine.

"And so you turned to Suzy," I said softly, pausing with a frown.

"Suzy was there," he admitted, the truth hanging heavy in the air as he grappled with his emotions.

"She didn't shy away from my touch. I was heartbroken, and I—" *Did he just stammer here?* "I needed someone to tell me everything was all right."

[179]

"Romeo," I began, my voice barely above a whisper, "love is not a game of chance where you simply roll the dice anew when fortune does not favor you." *Another quote I should send to Mercutio.* The thought shortly distracted me, and I felt a weird lurch deep inside my stomach.

"Isn't it?" Romeo's laugh was strained, forced. "Isn't that exactly what it is?"

"Perhaps," I conceded, "but some bets are too great, and the cost of losing too high."

"Well, at least I am still searching," he snapped back at me, his voice sharp, cutting through the quiet like a blade. "When was the last time you were looking for someone to love? Do you ever go on any dates anymore?"

His words stung, striking a chord deep within me, and for a moment, I felt an ache in my chest. When was the last time, indeed? I racked my brain. Whatever relationships I had were in the past, when I was still a kid, and nothing had been serious. Nothing recent. Nothing worth mentioning, and nothing to qualify me as a love doctor ready to give advice. Romeo was right. Who was I to lecture him about love? But I swallowed the hurt, pushing it down where it couldn't cloud my judgment.

"Maybe I am not an expert," I admitted, feeling the bitter truth settle on my tongue. "But I know enough to see the pattern, cousin."

"Pattern?" Romeo scoffed, his

defensiveness a tangible thing between us.

"Yes," I continued, my tone gentler now, a balm to the abrasiveness that hung between us. "You wanted to kiss Juliet, didn't you?"

His silence was answer enough, but he nodded anyway, a reluctant admission that carried the weight of his desires.

"But she told you no," I said, the statement hanging in the air like a specter of unfulfilled wishes.

"Suzy didn't say no." His voice was softer now, tinged with regret, or perhaps just resignation.

"And were you happy once you kissed her?"

Romeo was silent. Then, after a long pause, he shook his head.

"Cousin," I started carefully, as to make sure I didn't spook him with what I was about to say next. "Is it possible that neither of them is the right one for you?"

"What's that supposed to mean?" There was a fire in his eyes then, a spark that threatened to ignite into anger.

"Only that Suzy seemed more approachable when you felt lonely, perhaps even rejected. And Juliet... she seems more like a serious girl," I said, watching him closely, gauging his reaction.

"Serious?" he repeated, his voice a mix of

anger and something else, something that sounded like respect.

"Romeo," I began, the words catching in my throat, "perhaps it's time to consider what you truly want. And what you're willing to risk for it."

This made him fall silent, and for a moment, we stood opposite each other, each lost in our own thoughts.

I studied my cousin, his cheeks no longer as rosy as when he had first entered. The tension seemed to have left his muscles somewhat, and his whole posture started to become more relaxed.

"Yes," he then finally said, hesitating. "Yes, I think you are right."

*Good,* I thought, and let my shoulders relax a little. Had I finally gotten through to him?

"I'll make it up to her."

Perhaps I hadn't. That wasn't exactly what I meant when I told him to think about what he truly wanted.

"I'll write Juliet a sonnet, buy her roses, no, lilies, she loves lilies, and I'll apologize, properly."

My eyes narrowed at his words. *A sonnet and flowers?* It felt too superficial for a wound so deep.

"You think a few pretty words and

flowers will fix this?" My skepticism hung heavily in the air between us, mingling with the faint scent of my dinner, now forgotten.

"Ben, you don't understand," Romeo insisted, stopping only to lock eyes with me. "I think I need someone. And, like you said, she is serious. About us. About me."

"And you don't wish to look a little further? Perhaps step out of your comfort zone?" I murmured, but he didn't seem to catch my tone of ridicule.

"Are you suggesting I should start dating men?" He scoffed, running a hand down his face, but the flicker of doubt in his gaze told me my words had hit home. Silence settled over us, thick and unyielding, until I finally rose and peered outside once more. The street was empty.

"The coast is clear," I announced, my voice low. "If you still want to enact your genius master plan, I suggest you go home and write that sonnet."

Romeo nodded, determination steeling his features. I looked at him sideways and grinned because the thought of Romeo typing out a sonnet was too absurd for words. I could see Mercutio do such a thing. He had a way with words. But Romeo?

"I'm going to win her back, Ben. You'll see," Romeo said while he took a step closer, and by the tone of his voice, I could hear that he truly believed his own words. *Well, let him try.*

"By the way," I interrupted him, watching as he gently eased my window open. I pointed at it. "Why did you climb in through the window? Why not use the door like normal people do?"

A sheepish smile slipped on Romeo's lips as he turned away from the window to face me.

"Er, she might have been chasing me," he stammered, which made me raise a brow because there was another untold story here. *Did I even want to know?*

"Who? Juliet?" I asked because, *yes*, I did want to know so I could share the juicy news with the rest of the group. *Mercutio first.*

But Romeo was already shaking his head.

"Nah," he said, biting his lip as I looked at him, confused. "Want to guess again?"

"You don't mean...?" I gasped, realizing it must have been Suzy. Romeo nodded when he saw the understanding dawn in my eyes. *Of course, she must have been angry as well.* I could just picture the chase. "Suzy that bad?"

"Oh, no! She wasn't angry," Romeo laughed nervously and fidgeted with his jacket. At least he was wearing one today. "I mean," he started, stammering, "Suzy was kind of, you know, chasing me to finish what we started."

I looked at him dumbfounded, which prompted him to continue, "I just didn't want

[184]

her to, uh, catch me heading back home."

*Huh?* So Romeo had run away from a girl who had wanted to kiss him? That was a first.

"So you decided to climb up my drain?"

"Perhaps?" Romeo was still smiling sheepishly, but I had heard enough silly tales.

I stepped in front of him and deliberately closed the window, watching his face as he followed my every move. He looked at me in surprise while I folded my arms in front of my chest, making myself appear a little broader and more intimidating.

"The door," I ordered, and it took a moment before Romeo seemed to comprehend what I meant. His eyebrows lifted, and he turned on his heels.

"Of course," he said, hurrying over to the door of my apartment. With a chuckle, I opened it for him.

"Were you really going to climb out of my window?"

*The thought was hilarious.*

"Perhaps," Romeo said with an embarrassed tone. He stopped in the doorway to pull me in for a hug.

"Thank you for listening to me, Ben." His voice was a low whisper. For a moment, I closed my eyes and basked in his warmth. Romeo's hugs were nice. Not my favorite, but still welcome. When he finally pulled apart, he flashed me a smile, which I returned.

"Go on then," I said, "Go write your sonnet, *Shakespeare*. But think about what you want, Romeo."

Which was advice that went against the ancient-old saying. *Follow your heart*.

But hey, love is about both hearts involved. I wasn't a love doctor, but I knew as much as that. And I slowly started to wonder if Romeo's heart truly led him to all these disastrous dates. Or was he perhaps covering up something? Something his heart wanted, but he was somehow denying?

With one last look, Romeo stepped into the hallway. I watched him as he rounded the corner, then closed the door and made my way to the window. I waited until he appeared below me, just to make sure he got away safely. I watched as he slipped out into the night. As soon as he disappeared, I reached for my phone, the cool surface a stark contrast to the warmth of my palm.

*"You'll never guess what just happened..."* I typed to Mercutio, eager to share the tale. The message disappeared, and a few seconds later, a ping signaled a new message had come in.

Mercutio had replied with just three words.

*"Romeo and Juliet?"*

# *Eleven*

Now that Romeo had left, the energy in my apartment buzzed with giddiness as I sat there, eagerly typing away on my phone. Mercutio already seemed to be completely up to date. *How did he do that*, I wondered? How did he always seem to know what was going on in everyone's life?

At least he joked about it, which made me feel slightly better about the entire situation. I couldn't help but grin as I scrolled through his recent messages. I was trying to keep my cool and pretended that I wasn't eagerly awaiting whatever message he would send me next. I didn't want to seem overly eager.

*Respect him, Benvolio,* I reminded myself. *Respect that Mercutio needs time to type.*

But that time seemed to stretch, and no answer came. *Mercutio is typing,* my app kept reminding me. My eyes were focused on my screen up to the point where I forgot to blink.

Sometimes the typing indicator disappeared, but no new message arrived. I felt my heart sink. And then it appeared again, and I let out a sigh of relief. *What on earth was he going to say that took this long*? I started to get more and more nervous.

A new message popped up on my screen.

*Romeo.*

*"Thanks again,"* he merely said, and I let out a sigh. He had arrived home.

*"Go write that sonnet,"* I replied, then looked at the contacts in my phone.

Mercutio was still typing.

I desperately needed a distraction. My eye fell on Juliet's name. We had exchanged quite a few messages since we swapped numbers. She'd mostly asked me about things Romeo liked. Such as his favorite food, flowers, and hobbies. But sometimes, we talked about things she enjoyed and discovered that we had things in common. I had to admit that I liked her even more now that I had gotten to know her better. And knowing what Romeo had done to her made me feel bad for her.

I hesitated for just a moment before my fingers eagerly tapped out a message.

*"Are you all right?"* I sent it off into the void, hoping to distract myself from the restless longing for Mercutio's message. But he was still typing.

Juliet's reply came swiftly. *"How do you know what happened?"* Juliet's text read, a line so simple yet laden with unspoken hurt. I sensed the betrayal that must have clenched her heart.

How did I know what had happened? Well, I knew because Romeo had made a run for it and climbed into my home like a burglar. *But I*

[188]

*couldn't tell her that, could I?* I didn't want to sound like an accomplice to Romeo's stupidity and lose what little trust Juliet had in me.

"*I saw Romeo,*" I admitted. It was the truth, but only a sliver of it.

"*Something happened,*" Juliet confirmed. Her message was short. I imagined her, the phone lighting up her face as she hovered above the screen. She had to be angry with him.

"*It's okay if you don't wish to talk about it. But know that I am here if you need someone to rant to.*" I typed, fingers hesitating before sending the message.

My phone seemed to grow heavier with each passing second. Mercutio had stopped typing, but no new message had appeared. I frowned.

Then Juliet was typing again. I could see that Romeo was still online, but he was quiet. I wondered if he was chatting with Juliet as well.

"*Romeo... he's not serious about us,*" Juliet's text appeared, overlapping my screen. I clicked on it to read the rest of the message. "*Caught him with someone else. He kept saying I was special, but apparently, I am just another girl to him.*"

"*That is horrible,*" I replied, the glow of the screen casting shadows across my face. Horrible, but completely expected. I let out a sigh before I worried my lip, my eyes drifting to the wall as I thought about how to phrase the

[189]

next bit.

*"What an ass."*

Not brought with tact, but it conveyed how I felt about my cousin at the moment.

*"Thanks, Benvolio. That means a lot, especially coming from you,"* Juliet wrote back, punctuating her gratitude with a smiley face. *Yeah, she thought he was an ass as well.* I had to stifle a chuckle.

In an attempt to make us both feel better, I changed the subject to something lighthearted.

*"Have you heard about that guy at the park who tried to skate down the half-pipe and ended up faceplanting?"* I chuckled, remembering the hilarious sight. *"I've got the video around here somewhere. Wait, let me send it to you."*

*"Oh no, not another one!"* Juliet joined in with laughter according to the emojis she sent me, then another message popped onto my screen once she had watched the video. *"Who filmed this? Was that Mercutio I heard laughing?"*

I smiled broadly. *"Yes. One of his friends at the park. He hopes the video will go viral."*

Juliet was typing and a new message appeared. *"I'll send it to all my friends then."*

She was a good one. I didn't understand why Romeo had gone and screwed it all up. Casting another glance at my chat list, I could tell Romeo was still online. But the swiftness of Juliet's replies told me she wasn't talking to him.

[190]

I sincerely hoped he wasn't chatting with Suzy.

*"And did you hear this?"* I typed to Juliet again, seeing as she was the only one replying at the moment. Mercutio's chat was still glaringly empty, and Romeo's presence was like a ghost hovering online. There, but silently. *"Paris, you know him? Exchange student? Came to Verona recently? He tried to impress a girl by serenading her outside her window with his guitar. But he got the wrong window and ended up serenading her grandma instead."*

*"Classic Paris! Maybe he'll find true love with that granny instead,"* she quipped, and for a moment, I could imagine her smiling brightly on the other side. Then, a new message appeared.

*"Did you know Paris asked me out on a date?"*

For a moment, I was speechless, then sent a reply. *"No?"* A pause. *"What happened?"*

*"I turned him down and chose to go out with Romeo instead."*

I sat back and had to read her message a second time. *Did she truly choose Romeo over granny-serenading Paris?* I wasn't sure which of the two sounded like the worst choice.

She was typing. Sending her message took her long enough for me to get up and fill a glass of water, then return to my spot on the couch before her reply finally came in. *"Stupid, I*

[191]

know."

I smiled faintly at that and sent her a reassuring text back. *"Not that stupid. We all make mistakes."* The smiley I added earned me another laughing face in return, this time with tears streaming from the smiley's eyes. At least she wasn't feeling so bad anymore.

As I thumbed my phone, idly scrolling through the contacts, that familiar twinge of conscience pricked at me. I paused at Rosaline's name.

*"Juliet,"* I began, typing with deliberation, *"I know we're having fun and all. But there's someone who might understand what you're going through better than I can."* The letters traveled across the digital space between us. *"Rosaline. She's been where you are."* Well, sorta. She'd never been in love with Romeo, but I didn't need to mention that. *"Would you like me to send her number to you? I am sure she wouldn't mind if you contacted her. I know she likes you."*

Did Juliet even know that Romeo had been chasing Rosaline only weeks ago?

Her reply came quicker than I had imagined. *"Thank you, Benvolio. I'll reach out to her."*

I sent her Rosaline's number, then gave Rosaline a heads up about what had happened and that she could expect a message from Juliet soon. Rosaline nearly instantly replied that Juliet had already sent her a message. And then the chat between me and Juliet grew silent.

I let myself sink into the cushions of my couch, closing my eyes and taking a deep breath while I pinched my brow. Such a tumultuous evening it had been. A glance at the clock told me it wasn't even that late yet, but it felt like it had been hours since Romeo had come stumbling into my home.

Via the window. *Tusk*.

My phone erupted with the sudden trill of an incoming call, banishing the quietude. Mercutio's name flashed on the screen, igniting a spark that set my heart alight.

"Hey," I answered, voice hitching slightly with a cocktail of anticipation and relief.

"Ben! You sound as if you've been brooding over there!" Mercutio's voice, vibrant as the fuchsia streaks in his hair, cascaded through the speaker. I frowned.

"I was having a good time until a moment ago," I quipped, not entirely lying.

"Good time with whom, eh?"

I rolled my eyes and leaned a little forward on the couch, resting my elbows on my knees.

"Seriously? I was just chatting with Romeo, Juliet, Rosaline, and you."

"Ah, so you were just chatting up the girls *and* boys?"

[193]

"Very funny, Merc."

His laughter, uninhibited and infectious, filled the room. "Just your average Tuesday evening then?"

"Something like that. How about you?" I asked in turn. "Conquered any parkour challenges today?"

"Only the urban jungle, my friend. You should've seen it! The grace of a cat, the precision of a hawk!" he boasted, and I could almost see the dramatic flourish he would have accompanied those words with.

"Or the delusions of a peacock?" I suggested, the words woven with fondness and a touch of mischief.

"Touché," he said, and the sound of his chuckle was like a wonderful melody.

"So," I started, hesitating while I brushed my index finger past my thumb nervously. "Why did you call?"

"Mind if I swing by?"

A sigh of relief unfurled from within me. "I'd like that," I admitted, closing my eyes while I already imagined him here by my side. The idea of his presence, so full of sparkle and color, was always one to look forward to.

"Great! I'll be there in a jiffy," he assured me, and the call ended.

I stared at my table, halfway across the room. I hadn't bothered to clean up the dishes,

[194]

so I did so quickly. I didn't want Mercutio to stumble upon a messy apartment.

While I was cleaning, the doorbell rang, and I pushed the buzzer. Not much later, a knock resonated on the door. When I swung the door open, Mercutio's vibrant form stood illuminated on the threshold, a figure carved from vitality itself. The fuchsia — *still pink, in my opinion* — hue of his hair was a banner of defiance against the monochrome backdrop of the dull hallway. His deep brown eyes sparkled with an inner fire.

"Hey there, stranger," he greeted, his smirk holding a promise of mischief.

"Mercutio," I breathed out his name, and the corners of my lips twitched upward. Then he pulled me in for a hug.

This was the second time I was hugged by a friend today, but this time, it felt all the better. Like I said before, Romeo's hugs were fine, but Mercutio's were undeniably the best.

His laughter spilled into the space between us, filling my apartment with a warmth that radiated from the walls to the ceiling, a sun trapped within four corners. As he stepped inside, the world outside ceased to exist. His energy was infectious, and so was his joy.

"Shall we?" He gestured toward my bed in the corner of the room, and I frowned.

"I am not propositioning you, jeez,"

Mercutio cried out, rolling his eyes, and I couldn't help but chuckle and shake my head at that. "I just thought your bed is nicer to sit on than that old couch you still haven't thrown out."

I grinned while I watched him take place on my bed, *a mental image I hoped to never forget.* "You mean, I still haven't replaced it yet? Because a new couch costs money? And I am a poor student who can't afford any luxuries right now."

Mercutio rested his arms behind his head and let out an exaggerated sigh. "Yeah, that's it, Princess. I would even buy one for you if you just let me spoil you."

Something in my eyes started to glint when he said that, my stomach doing flip-flops. "You're already spoiling me too much, Mercutio."

The world narrowed to the softness of the blankets and the weightlessness of laughter as I settled onto my bed, next to Mercutio. A fortress padded with pillows in every imaginable shade of blue. When he hit me with one of my pillows, playfully, I picked up another and hit him back. Before we knew it, we were both laughing.

"I am spoiling you?" Mercutio asked, his voice a little too loud and a little too joyful.

I was already buried underneath him, the

pillow repeatedly coming down on top of my head, smothering my laughter as I shouted that I surrendered. He finally let me breathe again, stopping his assault but not getting off of me.

He remained on top of me for a little longer, lean body pressed warm and gentle against my own. *It felt good.* Our eyes locked, and I saw the corners of his lips curl into a soft smile.

Then he finally pushed himself up, and the moment was broken.

"Let's play a game," he then said, scrambling off the bed to get the controllers out. "I can't wait to beat you in one of these."

"You can certainly try," I said, grinning widely as I watched him set up the game. "But I'm sure I've put in a lot more hours than you have."

Mercutio faked a gasp, and I had to chuckle again. "Blasphemy!" he then shouted. Prepare for defeat, Benvolio. My hand is unstoppable."

"Until you get a repetitive strain injury," I muttered, which earned me another fake gasp. Our laughter mingled once again.

"You're silly," Mercutio finally whispered as we both caught our breaths again. His hand slipped to my knee, and I watched his fingers grasp the fabric of my jeans, squeezing lightly. "But the evening is young, and I can't wait to take you on."

I smiled at him. "Then show me what you've got, Cutio."

Mercutio's dark eyes twinkled.

As the hours slipped by unnoticed, the game became less about winning, and we got distracted by talking about friends we knew and silly videos we had seen on the internet. Mercutio got us some drinks out of my fridge, and I provided him with snacks, which was easy. I didn't need to ask if he was hungry or what taste he fancied. I knew him like the back of my hand, and I watched him gobble down handfuls of sweets and snacks with a grateful expression. The game was switched for another while time ticked by. And when we got too tired, the game console was switched off, and Mercutio pulled me down onto the bed with him. The laughter had faded, but the warmth it left behind swathed us like an invisible blanket.

He groaned. "It's getting late," a murmur from his lips that betrayed misery. He didn't want to leave, and neither did I want to see him go.

"You can stay over?" I suggested, not willing to move when his warm body was pressed next to mine.

"Like a sleepover?" Mercutio murmured, probably already half asleep. I felt his arm drape over me but decided to remain quiet, afraid I

[198]

might scare him off if he realized it.

"Yeah," I murmured while I studied his face. His eyes were closed, his lips slightly parted. From this angle, I could see how long his lashes were. The mop of fuchsia-colored hair was draped on the pillow, blending in nicely with the blue of my bed. *Like a true sleeping beauty*, I thought, but I didn't dare to voice it out loud. He was enchanting like this, a wonderful sight.

I watched the rise and fall of his chest. The breaths he took were slower now, deeper. My hand reached out, hesitant and trembling, and then I brushed a strand of hair away from his face with quivering fingers. The strands slipped through my fingers like silk.

"Mercutio," I whispered, though no further words followed. My chest was at peace that night.

No petals came forth.

# *Twelve*

It had been a while since I last had a coughing fit. It meant I didn't have to feel so bad about postponing that visit to the doctor. The sink stared back at me, pale and thankfully empty. I traced my fingers along the smooth porcelain, thinking of all the petals I'd retched into its basin over the past few weeks. Their velvety softness always startled me at first, deceiving me into thinking the disease wasn't so bad. But the metallic tang of blood that followed snapped me back to reality.

I hadn't vomited any petals for a week now. A foolish part of me clung to hope that I was somehow getting better. But the ever-present ache in my chest whispered that I could be wrong.

I didn't want to think of it, and so I sighed, turning my eyes away from the sink. I had to stop dwelling on what-ifs and maybes. Mercutio would be here any minute, and I needed to make myself presentable.

Glancing at the mirror, I saw my reflection staring back at me. Pale skin, tousled blond curls still dripping water, eyes ringed by shadows that even the best concealer couldn't hide. For all my efforts to look healthy, the disease still left its mark.

But I managed a faint smile as I combed my hair and picked out a smart light blue shirt. Just because I looked ill didn't mean I couldn't still take some pride in my appearance.

The smile grew into a grin as a knock sounded at the door, followed by Mercutio barging in with his usual hurricane of energy. His fuchsia hair and denim jacket with the large letters of *MONTAGUE* on the back made my heart flutter traitorously.

"Ready to go out, Bennieboy?" He swept into an elaborate bow, pink strands falling rakishly over one eye. I watched him as he dipped low, my gaze following the skin of his knees peeking through the stylish tears in his jeans.

"With you? Always." I hoped the sincerity in my voice wasn't too obvious. But the beaming smile Mercutio gave me in return made even the ever-present ache seem to fade, if only for the moment.

Mercutio's arm settled around my shoulders as we headed out into the bustling city streets, his touch sending little thrills through me. I breathed in the scent of his cologne, something rich and spicy that suited him perfectly, and I relished his warm touch, allowing myself to sink a little closer into him.

We chatted and laughed easily, Mercutio regaling me with an increasingly absurd tale

[201]

about his run-in with some Capulets the other day. He didn't mention Tybalt, for which I was grateful. Although the mental image of Mercutio trapped in Tybalt's arms in the darkness of the night was still burned into my mind. But I was slowly starting to believe that it had truly meant nothing to him. If it had, Mercutio would have told me by now. He would at the very least have spent time with him, right? Instead, he had been staying at my place for most of the week, visited me at my job, and constantly texted me.

Mercutio told me another funny tale about a run he did the other day, jumping from a building to a wall, and how he had taught himself a new trick to catch himself if he lost his balance during the run. I was content to simply listen to the rise and fall of his voice, appreciating his flair for dramatic storytelling.

Lost in our conversation, we almost didn't notice Romeo until he popped up right behind us.

"And hello to you!" he called out cheerily. He flung his arms around us, pushing himself in between, like a kid breaking up his parents. It was embarrassing, and I instantly regretted having lost Mercutio's warmth.

Mercutio frowned at Romeo as if he, too, was displeased by our friend's rather abrupt interruption. His expression was enough to make me chuckle.

[202]

"So, where are we going?" Romeo asked.

"*We*," and Mercutio stressed the word to indicate that it excluded Romeo, who didn't seem bothered in the least by this. "*We* were on our way to have a drink. You, on the other hand, seemed to have lost your date."

Romeo's cheeks started to flush, and I wanted to roll my eyes. *Here we go again*, I thought, looking up at the sky above while I felt Romeo's arm tense around my shoulder. I silently wished Mercutio's arm had still been there, that I could still feel his rough jacket and smell his unique fragrance.

"I wasn't," Romeo hesitated, and I let out an audible sigh. He cast me an annoyed glare, as if he were angry I had interrupted him. "I was not waiting for a date. That's all I wanted to say," he clarified.

"No date?" Mercutio's voice was over the top and a delicious treat to listen to. He shook himself out of Romeo's arm and dramatically placed a hand on his own chest as if he were hurt. "What is this sacrilege I hear of? Romeo without a date?"

"Yeah, it does happen," Romeo answered while smiling sheepishly. He tried to avoid our eyes, giving the impression that there was more that he wasn't telling us.

I wondered who he had been waiting for. Juliet? Or Suzy?

[203]

I'd been exchanging messages with Juliet, not many, but still enough to know how she was doing. Romeo was rarely mentioned in her messages. Instead, she focused on her studies and her conversations with Rosaline. It seemed that the two girls got along just fine. Juliet's messages seemed livelier and more upbeat these days. Whether or not she ended up rekindling her romance with Romeo, bringing these two girls together had been a good move. Which reminded me…

"Did you ever deliver that sonnet you wrote for Juliet?"

At the mention of her name, Romeo's face fell ever so slightly before he smoothed his features back into an easy smile. "Alas, her heart remains elusive as ever."

"Which translates as…?"

"Which means she isn't interested in him," Mercutio clarified.

I nodded in understanding. An awkward beat passed between us before Mercutio clapped his hands decisively.

"Right, I have seen a fancy little café," he declared. "We just simply have to try it. It's got cats and everything."

A laugh erupted from Romeo, and I couldn't help but chuckle as well.

"Of course," I said. The cat café, the newest in Verona. Mercutio couldn't resist going there even if we tried to shackle him down and tie the heaviest weights to his feet. He would somehow break free, get in there, and take as many pictures with the cats as he could, then upload them all to his social media. His followers were going to love those pictures.

I shook my head, chuckling. "Incorrigible," I murmured.

"Well?" Mercutio asked, already skipping ahead of us by a few steps. "Are you coming or?"

"We're coming," Romeo and I readily agreed. Romeo's arm slid from my shoulder as he caught up with Mercutio. The two of them easily chatted about the weather while I was a few steps behind, taking in my surroundings. I was so caught up in my thoughts that I completely missed the moment when Mercutio tore himself away from Romeo's side to join me. Linking arms, we strolled down the cobblestone street, his bright smile directed fully at me.

"You're gonna meet the kittens," he said, grinning widely, while Romeo fell back into track with us.

"I'm going to show you the sweetest pussies in town!" Mercutio happily exclaimed, loud enough for everyone in the vicinity to hear.

Embarrassed, I groaned and tried to shield my face from the public. An impossible feat when Mercutio pinned my arm to my side

[205]

with his own, leaving me with only one hand to hide behind. Romeo distanced himself from us a little more, possibly pretending he wasn't part of the group. Everyone in Verona seemed to know we were Montagues and belonged together. But I understood his effort to try and get away from Mercutio's embarrassing double entendre.

"Quit it," I hissed, but playfully, earning me a pat on my shoulder from Mercutio, who started laughing out loud, obviously pleased with himself. "I'm not as interested in pussies as you are."

"Is that so?" Mercutio challenged me, raising a brow and pursing his lips. "Want to test that theory?"

I hummed thoughtfully. "You plan to *purr-plex* me?" I joked, stretching the purr deliberately.

His laughter was loud enough to draw attention, and a figure stepped directly into our path, forcing us to an abrupt halt. My breath caught as I recognized Tybalt's scowling face. His cold eyes bored into mine, full of unspoken threats. I knew why he had sought me out.

*I wasn't supposed to be with Mercutio.*

A command I had willfully ignored.

And now he had spotted us together, arms linked and laughing.

This wasn't good. With a bit of luck, Tybalt would be all bark and no bite. But I feared that the chance of him simply scolding and threatening us, and leaving it at that, was very slim.

I swallowed, my throat suddenly dry, and felt how Mercutio tensed by my side, but he didn't let go of me. Our arms still linked, his grip on me possibly even tighter. To our side, a few feet away, Romeo had blended in with the people who were just passing by, hiding himself away from Tybalt's eyes as he tried to measure the situation.

I didn't blame him for taking his distance. An encounter with Tybalt was always tense, but we all knew that if anyone could diffuse it, it was me. And if it came to a fight, then the only one who could win a hand-to-hand fight was Mercutio. In a confrontation with Tybalt, we were the best and safest bet.

Usually.

But that was before Tybalt caught feelings for Mercutio. For the first time, the thought that this could end badly crawled into the back of my mind. *How to get away unscathed*?

"Well, well," Tybalt purred, his dark eyes resting on Mercutio, gaze smoldering. "If it isn't my favorite Montagues out for a stroll."

Though his words were cordial, tension sang through every line of his body. Then his eyes slid to me. I met his gaze unflinchingly, refusing to show weakness. Mercutio shifted

[207]

uneasily beside me, sensing the animosity simmering beneath the surface.

I realized neither of my friends was aware of Tybalt's threat to me. They didn't know he was after me specifically, that he had promised to beat me so badly I wouldn't be a pretty boy any longer. *Not that I felt like I was one now.* But I wasn't keen on finding out how far he would take things.

Tybalt moved closer, crowding into my space. "I thought I told you to stay away," he hissed under his breath so only I could hear. His hand drifted toward the hilt of his knife in warning. *So he was armed.* I wasn't surprised, but had hoped he would leave the weapon out of it.

I held Tybalt's furious gaze, acutely aware of Mercutio standing tense and confused beside me. His arm left mine.

"What's all this about?" Mercutio finally burst out, unable to bear the charged silence any longer.

Tybalt rounded on him. "Stay out of this, Mercutio," he snapped. "This business is between your lover boy and me."

Mercutio's eyes widened in shock. "What?"

I was thinking the same. *What?* What had he just called me?

*Wasn't* he *the one secretly dating Mercutio?*

"Enough!" I said sharply, cutting him off.

[208]

*You have misunderstood,* I wanted to say, but somehow, the words wouldn't come forth.

Beside me, Mercutio stood, a deep frown once again marring his features. He looked like he was about to say something, but I was quicker, stepping in front of him to draw his attention away.

"You threatened to bash my face in if I didn't stay away from Mercutio," I revealed, my eyes firmly upon Tybalt. I felt Mercutio's heat burn into my back, felt his intense eyes upon me as he must be wondering what I was doing.

"But I can't stay away."

*Mercutio is my best friend,* I wanted to say, but my tongue felt heavy and my mouth dry. *I wish he could be more than that.*

"Benvolio," I heard my name behind me, how it slipped breathlessly from Mercutio's lips. I made the error of turning ever so slightly to look at him, only to find I couldn't bear it. Not when he was looking at me through his lashes like *that.* So soft, so vulnerable.

A look Tybalt couldn't have missed.

I snapped my head back to the Capulet in front of me while I felt another tug deep inside my stomach. Mercutio was attractive, without a doubt. No wonder someone like Tybalt desired him. No wonder I... *No, don't finish that thought.*

"I've seen the two of you. That night," I confessed, squeezing my eyes shut as I forced the words out through gritted teeth, each syllable paining me. *Was I truly going to do this?*

"Outside of Mercutio's home. Kissing. Touching."

I took another deep breath, mindless of the way Tybalt glowered at me and cracked his knuckles, ready to take the punch. He looked pained to hear my words, so I closed my eyes again so I wouldn't have to see the conflict in his eyes. I felt Mercutio's soft hand hot upon my arm, anchoring me, vying for my attention. But I had to do this.

"If the two of you are dating, then I will accept that and wish for nothing but your happiness."

*There.* It was out in the open. I had said it.

I felt Mercutio's arm grow slack, then felt it slip away from mine. I slowly opened my eyes and took a deep breath to calm myself. I hoped that Mercutio would still want to be friends with me.

With Mercutio no longer holding me, Tybalt took his chance, stepping forward and shoving me hard in the chest. I felt the handle of the knife press painfully into my ribs.

"Liar!" he spat, his words laced with venom. "You think the world is your stage and we will just believe whatever pretty words you say? That you would accept it? Don't make me laugh. 'I'll accept it'," he imitated my voice, making it sound high-pitched and shrill, mocking me.

"You're such a bad actor, saying you won't mind." The handle of the knife pressed uncomfortably against my side, a silent reminder that he could easily turn the sharp object around and pierce my skin.

"You think you're such a saint? That you are immune to feelings like disgust or… *jealousy*?" he taunted, leaning in dangerously close until I could feel his hot breath on my face.

"Drop the act."

He paused before his voice lowered, the words spoken through gritted teeth. "You think you've seen it all, but you've seen nothing, you hear me, Montague? Nothing."

And I didn't know how to react, because how could I call their kiss '*nothing*' when a kiss from Mercutio would mean the world to me?

"But I," here Tybalt hesitated, his tongue peeking out from between his lips as he pressed it against his molars. I felt the back of the knife press deeper into my stomach, a silent warning.

"I've seen the way you look at him," his voice dropped low again, lips curling in disgust.

I stood frozen. I didn't know what to say.

Mercutio's laughter caught Tybalt off guard. In his confusion, Tybalt released his grip on me. He turned to Mercutio with a look of disbelief, while I exhaled a sigh of relief when the knife was no longer pressed against me.

"You can't be serious," Mercutio chuckled, "All of this is because you're jealous?" His laughter only grew louder.

Tybalt's body was tense, his posture rigid like the sharp edge of a blade. But he did not deny it. The sneer that clung to his features was a mask of hate, drawn tight across the canvas of his face. His nostrils flared with suppressed rage. Every muscle in his form seemed taut, ready to spring. Yet, he stayed silent, not even humoring Mercutio with a grunt or a groan.

So Mercutio was right then?

I could feel Mercutio shift beside me, his body language a stark contrast to Tybalt's. He was fluid where Tybalt was stiff, an amused smirk playing on his lips as if he found the entire confrontation to be a silly performance put on just for his entertainment. *He didn't know how serious Tybalt was*, I thought, alarmed. He was probably flattered that Tybalt was prepared to fight over him. The same way knights dueled each other to win the princess in romantic fairy tales. Like I said before, Mercutio was always a dreamer, and he loved a good fairytale.

My eyes sought Romeo and I noticed how more and more people began to slow their pace and started to mutter and whisper, their eyes drawn to us. Montagues and a Capulet. Everyone in Verona knew this would climax into

[212]

a fight.

"Oh, Tybalt, you fool, you thought that kiss meant something?" Mercutio taunted with a wink. I inwardly cried out for him to stop. Of course, silly, wonderful Mercutio had no idea how serious Tybalt was. How much salt he was rubbing into the Capulet's wounds. "You never stood a chance at claiming my heart."

His words were enough. Tybalt trembled with fury, his knuckles white around the handle of his knife. It looked like part of him had shattered. As if Mercutio's taunting words had broken something vital in the young man.

We were all waiting for him to react, for the inevitable storm that was to follow. From the corner of my eye, I noticed that Romeo had silently moved closer to us and shifted uneasily, ready to intervene if needed. His dark eyes were fixed on Tybalt's hand, waiting to see if Tybalt would actually use the weapon.

By the hushed whispers of the people around us, I could tell that at least some of them had noticed how Tybalt held the knife. I silently prayed one of them would call the police, but I had the nagging feeling that they were waiting. Confrontations between Capulets and Montagues weren't a rarity. They seemed to expect that this confrontation would end like all others.

Mercutio placed his hand on his hip and

shook his head. "Tybalt, Tybalt," he started with a smirk, and I could already tell this was going to be bad. I silently pleaded with Mercutio to stop provoking him. Had he not seen the knife?

But Mercutio didn't seem to notice. His sing-song voice betrayed that something was about to follow that would upset the Capulet even more. He moved gracefully in front of our shared enemy, as smooth and fluid as a seasoned performer, every action a clear provocation.

"Did you really believe that updating your status would magically make it true? That I would suddenly want to be with you?"

Mercutio's movements came to an abrupt halt, and his dark eyes, full of fire, locked with Tybalt's. His lips curved into a twisted grin. "That kiss was just a little taste. And it confirmed that I'll never want you as my boyfriend."

*Shit, no. He had not just said that, had he?* Although a rush of pride filled me upon hearing Mercutio stand up for himself like that, at the same time, I felt dread fill my every vein. Because Mercutio taunting Tybalt while he already had his hand on his knife meant that things could get serious.

*Seriously dangerous.*

I took a deep breath, trying to keep my voice steady despite the fear pounding through me. I spread my arms, one in the direction of Mercutio to hopefully shush him and the other toward Tybalt in the hope of catching his attention. His silence was unnerving, especially as I could tell he was seething. Tybalt was someone who exploded at the slightest displeasure. But where was his anger now? Contained?

*Don't make me laugh.*

"Tybalt, please, let us discuss this rationally," I implored, holding my hands up in a gesture of peace. "There is no need for violence between us."

But I should have known that Tybalt was beyond reason now. His jealousy and pride were wounded. With a guttural cry, he lunged forward, backhanding me hard across the face with the handle of his knife. I stumbled, the force of the blow sending me tumbling to the floor as pain exploded through my cheek.

*Had he just struck me with the blunt end of his knife?* It was a small mercy amidst the agony. *He could have lashed out and slashed me,* I thought, pushing down the panic that was rising inside of me. But a shadow fell over me before I could give it any more thought. When I looked up, Mercutio was looming over me, looking down at me in concern. He offered his hand for me to take, ready to help me back up to my feet.

I looked over his shoulder, worried that

Tybalt would lunge at us. But Romeo was already there, shoving Tybalt back.

"How dare you strike Benvolio," he thundered. Though shorter than Tybalt, Romeo drew himself up, radiating righteous fury. And Tybalt's expression was one of surprise, a look I had not seen on him often. He probably hadn't expected Romeo to be there, having stood hidden among the crowd. I could only hope Tybalt hadn't brought any of his lackeys. Even with the three of us, I felt like we were already heavily outnumbered.

I mean, Tybalt had a knife. *Dammit.*

Determined, I took Mercutio's hand, grateful for his tight grip on me as I stood up. Then I turned back to Tybalt.

"You better back away, or I will call the police." I threatened, hoping that someone already had done just that.

Romeo firmly positioned himself between us, acting as a human shield. I groaned inwardly, grateful for his attempt to defend me, yet worried that he might become the next target. We had been in fights before, but I had a particularly bad feeling about this one.

"Romeo," I whispered, and instantly reached for my sore cheek. Was it already getting swollen? My jaw hurt too much to allow full movement, and I silently cursed how inaudible his name had tumbled from my lips.

[216]

He probably hadn't heard it.

*Don't let this escalate*, I thought helplessly. I looked over at Mercutio, seeking his gaze, but his eyes were lowered, directed at Tybalt's right hand. I looked as well, only to feel my breath hitch in my chest. His knuckles were white on the knife, ready to strike.

Was he holding himself back?

Tybalt had bared his teeth. "Out of my way! This isn't about you."

But Romeo refused to budge. He turned his back on Tybalt, willfully ignoring him.

"Cousin, are you all right?" he asked, his worried gaze upon me.

I nodded, though my cheek throbbed. "I'm fine, Romeo. But you—"

Tybalt snarled, not allowing me the chance to finish my sentence and warn Romeo of the imminent danger he was in.

"Last chance, Montague. Step aside, or I'll gut you both!" Tybalt raised his hand, pointing the knife at Romeo's back, aiming directly at his heart.

The crowd gasped, shrinking back. *Someone better call that alarm number now.* But Romeo held firm, protectiveness etched in every line of his body. He stubbornly kept his eyes on me, his back exposed to Tybalt. He didn't see what I saw, how Tybalt rose behind him. Something dark glinted in his eyes, his gaze

[217]

unfocused and as deadly as the knife in his hand.

My heart pounded, fear and frustration churning within me. I had to stop this before it went too far.

Behind my cousin, I could see how Tybalt raised the knife, the blade glinting in the sunlight.

Too late.

I did not think. I just pushed Romeo behind me.

Then he struck.

# *Thirteen*

The sound that echoed through the street was that of tearing. Not just fabric, but something more substantial. Something warm and soft. *Flesh.*

Mercutio's eyes widened as he tumbled forward, his arms wrapping around Romeo in a mock semblance of a hug. Behind him, the towering figure of Tybalt stood, arm pushed forth, the hilt of the knife shielded from my view by Mercutio.

I felt a tightness in my chest where Mercutio's warm hands had been only seconds ago, pushing me aside.

The world seemed to pause, a frozen tableau of shock and horror. Mercutio had just thrown himself into the path of danger. Tybalt's arm had swung with lethal intent toward us, his eyes ablaze with a fury that sent chills down my spine. But it was Mercutio—brave, impulsive Mercutio—who had received the blow. That blade hadn't been meant for him, but it found its home in his flesh all the same.

"Mercutio!" I cried out, my voice barely rising above the crescendo of chaos that enveloped us.

His silhouette staggered backward, the wildness that always danced in his deep brown eyes now dulled by a haze of pain. He stood there, swaying slightly, his hand reaching toward the wound with an almost childlike curiosity. And then, the crimson reality bloomed across his palm, a stark contrast against the blue silk he so loved to wear and the blue denim jacket that was getting stained at an alarming rate.

"He actually did it," he gasped, his voice tinged with disbelief, "I didn't see that coming."

*I had.* I had already felt the plunge before Tybalt had taken it. But I hadn't expected Mercutio to be this swift, to push me aside and recklessly dive in between Tybalt and my cousin. We were the best of friends, so I probably should have expected it, should have known that Mercutio wouldn't stand idle. Why hadn't I been stronger, pushed him back? Why hadn't I acted?

Tybalt remained motionless, staring at the knife in his grasp as if it were a foreign object he couldn't recognize. His dark curls framed a face pale with shock, his slender frame rigid with the weight of what his anger had wrought.

"Mercutio, hold on," I pleaded, stepping forward to support him. But his knees buckled, bringing him crashing to the ground like a puppet severed from its strings.

"Damn..." Mercutio groaned as he sat there, the fuchsia of his hair now a stark contrast

[220]

to the pallor of his skin. A skin that had once been so alive, so warm of color. Blood seeped into his jacket, the word 'Montague' disappearing beneath a growing stain. It was as if the very essence of who he was—fashionable, energetic, fearless—was being drained away before my eyes. The name of my family disappeared, was swallowed by the red, until it looked like a gigantic red flower had blossomed on his back.

"Stay with me," I urged, my hands trembling as I hovered over him, desperate to undo this nightmare. Yet, all I could see was the severity of his wounds, the fabric of his clothes cleaved apart, the flesh beneath torn and angry.

"I had cats scratch me before," he tried to joke, though the quiver in his voice betrayed the agony he felt. "That's what this is," he hummed. "Just a scratch."

I could feel Romeo hover over us indecisively. Others came rushing toward us. Men and women, I didn't have time to study their faces. I could hear them, felt them as they brushed against me and helped me to stabilize Mercutio and press against the wound with whatever they could find. Mercutio was now on the cold, cobbled floor, his head on my lap as I tried to keep him here with me.

"Just from a bigger cat," Mercutio managed, but the joke was lost on me. Prince of

Cats or not, Tybalt did more than scratch him. He stabbed him. The wound looked serious, and Mercutio's voice dwindled and became weaker.

"Mercutio, don't talk like that," I said, fighting back a surge of despair. Mercutio was not going to die. Not like this. The tears that welled up in my eyes were forced back violently as I bit my lip, my hand tightening around his.

"Someone call an ambulance!" A voice cut through my thoughts, sharp and urgent. *It was my own.* Had I just called out for help? I had a phone, but I'd currently forgotten how to use one. I didn't want to let go of Mercutio's hand and miss how the warmth of his skin was slowly turning cold like the porcelain of my sink at home, the one I had held this morning as I prepared to go out and have drinks with him. Had that been only an hour or two ago? How had things gone astray this fast?

"Already done," someone else answered, though I scarcely heard them. *Help was coming,* was all my mind registered. That was good, right? I squeezed Mercutio's hand a little tighter. His scent slowly became lost amidst the metallic tang of blood.

My gaze fell upon Tybalt once more as he stood where he had been when he had raised the knife. He hadn't moved. I noticed faintly that no one had tried to wrestle the weapon from him or hold him down. I'd expected that. I'd expected people to jump on top of him and restrain him until the police arrived. But he stood all alone, the bloodied knife dangling in his hand. His eyes met mine, filled with a terror that mirrored my own.

A soft squeeze made me look down again at the friend whose head I cradled in my lap.

"Mercutio," I whispered, brushing a hand against his cheek, feeling the soft skin marred by the grit of the street and the heat of his blood. Fear gripped me. The fear of loss and the fear of a world without the light of his laughter.

"Curse them," Mercutio's words came out brittle and forced, like it took effort to speak. "Curse them and their stupid rivalry."

*Montagues. Capulets.* An endless fight. His lips parted in a silent gasp of pain, and he winced as someone put more pressure on him.

"Stay with me," I begged again, even as the sound of sirens wailed in the distance.

A tug at my hand again, and I forced a smile when it was difficult to do so. He looked up at me, not paying mind to the many hands that were pressing down on his chest in an attempt to stop the wound from draining him even more.

"I'm here," I whispered again. "Stay with me."

Mercutio's gaze met mine, a fleeting

[223]

connection that said everything words could not. His eyes, those deep pools of mischief, flickered with a pain he couldn't disguise. But he was still irrevocably Mercutio. Bold, unapologetic, alive.

But beneath that facade, I glimpsed the vulnerability of a boy who danced too close to the edge, whose laughter could not shield him from the sting of steel.

"Stay with me," I asked him silently, knowing he could tell from the movement of my lips what it was that I asked of him. He flashed me a careful smile, and then his grip on my hand grew slack. His shoulders slumped, and his lips parted.

His eyes fluttered closed.

I was pushed aside roughly by the elbow of a man I only vaguely recognized to be a paramedic. It was Romeo who had to pull me away so they could do their work. Their hands moved deftly, working to staunch the flow of red that seeped through Mercutio's clothes, painting him in hues of scarlet misery.

I swallowed hard, my throat tight with unshed tears and unsaid words. The voices of the paramedics were a blur, their commands floating meaninglessly as I fixated on the way Mercutio's chest moved. Too slow. Not at all.

*Was he still alive?*

The loud clatter of steel against the cobbles made me look up. In front of me, Tybalt stood, the same expression on his face as if he were frozen in time. *Why haven't the cops shown up yet?* His hands were covered in Mercutio's blood, but the knife was no longer there. I saw it glinting at his feet, the blade shimmering between the red of blood as it tainted the street below.

And then he turned abruptly. Tybalt moved so swiftly that those who stood around him had no time to intercept him. A loud shout of a man, *'Hey!',* but he ran for it. I watched Tybalt disappear, pushing himself with bloodied hands through the crowd until he was out of sight.

My heart pounded, a relentless drumbeat echoing the tumultuous thoughts swirling through my mind. The world around me dimmed to a narrow tunnel. The edges blurred with the chaos of paramedics weaving through the scene. There was my friend, pale and still, his vibrant spirit dimming as they hoisted him onto the stretcher, the fuchsia of his hair stark against the white sheet that seemed to swallow him whole.

"Mercutio," I whispered, my voice nothing but a breath lost in the cacophony. Fear clawed at my insides, tearing through the fabric of my composure. He was always so alive, so untouchable in his enthusiasm. To see him reduced to this fragile shell, shrouded in

[225]

sterility, was to witness the unthinkable.

"Can I… can I come with him?" My question was a plea to the paramedic securing the straps over Mercutio's chest, her face a mask of professional detachment.

"Only family," she replied curtly, not unkind but firm, shutting down the hope that had sparked within me.

*Family.* The word echoed hollowly as the ambulance doors closed with a definitive thud. Family was more than blood. It was the late-night confessions, shared laughter, and unspoken understanding. At that moment, I realized I had never felt more alone. I couldn't imagine a life without Mercutio in it.

The engine roared to life. As the vehicle pulled away, its lights swept across the street, illuminating the faces of those gathered around us, silently witnessing the display. We stood listlessly. Romeo, with his hands tangled in his curls, his eyes wide and haunted by the specter of guilt. And I, rooted to the spot, unsure of what to do next.

Someone pressed a hand to my shoulder. "Hey, are you okay?" I don't know how I responded. I can't recall if I even did.

"The police will be here soon," another said, offering to take me to the side of the road where Romeo had been ushered to already. For a moment, we stood there, together, with a crowd of people surrounding us, asking us if we needed anything.

Romeo's voice came across the chaos. "Go to him, Benvolio." It took me a moment before I realized he meant Mercutio, that I should follow him to the hospital. "Make sure he's all right. I'll deal with the cops, tell them what Tybalt did. You can always talk to them after."

His hands were a blur before my eyes, gestures wild and uncontrolled as his words tumbled over each other in a panic. I nodded, not trusting my own voice—a croak of grief lodged in my throat, tight and suffocating.

"He needs you," Romeo urged. "He needs one of us to be there with him, and I think it has to be you."

New sirens sounded, the police, as promised. What took them so long? I'd expect them to be here first. Perhaps they already had been. Was this just the backup? I hadn't focused on them.

My eyes fell on the discarded knife, bloodied and sinful, left alone by those around it so as not to meddle with the proof. It lay abandoned, an echo of violence that had unfolded with such swift brutality. Had he intended to kill Romeo with it? Had he wanted to kill me?

*Had he wanted to kill Mercutio?*

The blade was smeared with crimson, and my heart clenched. Behind me, policemen could be heard. They swarmed the area, a flurry of questions and commands ensnaring us in a web of procedure and suspicion.

I remembered Tybalt's expression. And when I looked up, I could see the ghostly trail where he had run and how the people had parted for him. It was a memory, but it was strong enough to know in which direction he had headed.

My chest heaved painfully as I wiped the corner of my lips with my sleeve. Standing up, I felt a strange sensation bubbling within me.

I had to *know.*

With deliberate steps, I carefully moved away from the weapon. I heard voices behind me, asking me to stay. I think I heard Romeo among them. But I no longer thought.

My feet carried me on their own, away from the spot that was covered in Mercutio's crimson red. The stain was now an ugly reminder of the horror that had taken place here, discoloring the cobbles of the street.

Away from the knife, blood spatters still stained the steel. Pink blossom petals had fallen on top, lightly brushing against the drying blood until they, too, ended up stained.

*I'd hardly noticed.* And as I ran, the wind carried the petals away.

# Fourteen

The cold wind whipped around me as I walked through the narrow alley that led to the canal, following Tybalt's trail. I clutched my jacket tightly to keep warm, my fingers felt numb. There was a coldness in my bones that I couldn't chase away, and each step I took was taken as in a dream. A nightmare. Not fully conscious.

*This couldn't be happening.*

Sunlight streamed through the gaps between the tall, old buildings, casting dappled shadows on the cobblestone path beneath my feet. I came to a halt when I saw Tybalt standing at the edge of the water. His tall, slender figure was illuminated by the soft afternoon light, creating a gentle glow around him. When I stepped toward him, he didn't turn, but his shoulders tensed, a subtle acknowledgment of my presence.

"Tybalt," I called out softly, approaching him with caution. He was no longer armed, but that didn't mean he couldn't lash out. Even if he stood there in silence, like a statue pensively overlooking the water.

His gaze remained fixed on the dark waters below, but he gave the slightest nod to acknowledge my presence. I hesitated, unsure of what to say or do next. It was rare to see Tybalt

[229]

so... vulnerable.

"Say it, Benvolio," Tybalt began, and I could hear the twinge of roughness in his voice. But sadness and defeat dominated, no matter how harsh and bitter he tried to make his words sound.

"Scold me," he continued. "Hit me. Make me bleed." *I deserve it*. But he did not voice it out loud. I had heard the underlying words, though. And I could see by the way he kept staring at the water, not bothering to even look at me, that he was lost in his own mind.

"Tybalt," I said again, my voice wavering. There were so many things I wanted to tell him. *I'm not here to fight you,* was one of them. But the words somehow wouldn't come out. It made me doubt my own thoughts and my own mind. Would I truly not hit him and kick him if I had the chance? I knew Romeo would have done that if he had been here in my place. He would have taken Tybalt's knife and returned the favor.

I had to shake that haunting thought away.

But I wasn't like my cousin. And even if anger and sadness were washing over me, making me feel numb and cold as if I'd been caught in the Winter's rain, I still wouldn't just run over to him and *kick the shit out of him*. That wasn't me. That wasn't helping Mercutio to stay alive.

"You stabbed him," I said instead. Although I wanted to ask 'why'. Why had he done it? Had he truly wanted to kill Romeo? And what for? Because Romeo had stood up for me?

Had he truly wanted to kill me? Why had he wanted to risk going to jail just to maim me, in front of Mercutio even?

Had he truly been acting out of jealousy?

But I didn't need to ask any of these questions, for Tybalt finally stirred. The movement was slight, just a tilt of the head so he could see me from the corners of his eyes. His body was still tense, his right hand hidden in the pocket of his jeans, the left resting on his upper thigh.

"I loved him, Benvolio. I truly did," his voice was low and laced with sadness. His confession shouldn't have taken me by surprise, but it still did, and I could feel my heart clench at the thought of Tybalt pining after Mercutio. Another unrequited love.

"I would never hurt him. Not like this. I—" he hesitated, his eyes drifting back to the water in front of him while his hands left his sides to tangle in his long curls. "I fucked up."

What could I say when my sworn enemy, or so he had led me to believe for nearly all my life, stood there, defeated, hands tangled in his

[231]

hair, tugging at the strands, eyes wide, and gaze distant? I looked at the tall Capulet speechlessly.

I wanted to believe him when he said he would never hurt Mercutio. *Except he had*. He had let himself be led by his rage, his anger, his jealousy, and all the ugly thoughts that must have been racing through his head. *Hot-headed*, the other Capulets called him. Fun in arguments, because he was easily riled up, but dangerous when a weapon was involved. Why had none of us seen this coming?

"*Damn you*. I hated you so much. Hated what you two have," Tybalt said, his eyes finally tracing back to me. I remained silent, listening.

"I tried to win him over, you know," Tybalt continued, his shoulders sagging slightly under the weight of his words. "But I knew, deep down, that I could never make him love me. He never even looked at me twice. Only to tease me, and I knew he wasn't serious when he did that. That I wasn't his type. That he'd rather spend his time with you."

He threw me another accusing glare, and I felt myself take an involuntary step back.

"You always distracted him from me," Tybalt's low voice murmured. Then his eyes dropped to the ground, and he looked away again, running a hand through his dark curls that were now unruly, as if a storm had tussled them around until they got tangled.

[232]

"Tybalt, I..." I started, struggling to find the right words. But he cut me off with a bitter laugh, turning his head ever so slightly to look at me from the corner of his eyes.

The cold wind brushed against my face, stirring my blond curls, but it was nothing compared to the icy knot that tightened in my chest.

Tybalt's voice had grown silent, his gaze drifting back toward the dark waters below. I could sense the weight of his thoughts pressing down on him, threatening to drown him in their depths. Slowly, he began to move, inching closer and closer to the edge of the canal. It took me a moment to realize what he intended, but when it struck me, a jolt of panic shot through my veins.

"Tybalt, wait!" I called out, my voice cracking as I reached for his arm. I hadn't even noticed I had run over to him. "Please, don't... don't do this."

He paused for an instant, his eyes meeting mine, but there was no warmth to be found in them, only the chill of despair. His lips curved into a bitter smile, one that held no trace of the haughty confidence I'd come to associate with the toughest Capulet in town.

"Mercutio is gone, Benvolio," he murmured, his voice barely carrying over the wind. "I killed him. I am a criminal now. A murderer. What reason have I left to live?"

[233]

My heart skipped a beat at the thought. Was he truly considering... *suicide?*

"Maybe... maybe he's not dead," I stammered, clinging to the faintest flicker of hope. My fingers dug into his jacket, holding him tightly and keeping him from moving any closer to the dreaded water behind him. "You don't know for sure. He might still... he might..."

His laugh cut through the air like a knife, sharp and cold. "You've seen him. How could he have survived that?" Tybalt pushed my hands away from him, his expression hardening. To my shock, I noticed a tear silently tracing its way down his cheek. "I murdered the boy I loved. There's nothing left for me here."

My mind raced, desperately searching for words to change his mind. Tybalt took my silence as a cue to start pushing me away. But my grip on his jacket remained and even tightened, not allowing him to get rid of me yet.

"You said it yourself. Mercutio didn't love you back. But there can always be another. Another love. Another chance. Please," I whispered, my voice barely audible even to my own ears. "Don't do this."

As if in answer to my plea, Tybalt's body tensed, and for an instant, I thought he might have changed his mind. But I could see it in his eyes, that fatal determination, the resolve to end his own life rather than face a world without

[234]

Mercutio. A hard push against my shoulders followed and sent me tumbling backward. Then, he launched himself toward the dark waters below.

"Tybalt!" I cried out as I regained my footing, immediately lunging forward to grab hold of him. Our bodies collided, and we fell to the ground, rolling dangerously close to the edge of the water, limbs tangled and hearts pounding a desperate rhythm.

"Let go of me!" Tybalt hissed while struggling beneath my grasp. But I held on, pinning him to the cold, damp stones of the canal's edge, my heart thundering in my chest like a wild beast trapped within a cage.

I wasn't a fighter, never had been. But I would fight him for this. I'd fight for his life. No matter if he always said he was the enemy. No matter, he wanted me dead just a moment ago.

I knew what love felt like, how desperate it could make you feel. Like him, I didn't want to imagine a life without Mercutio. But I also knew that the bad faded over time, that hurt could grow less sore, and wounds could heal when treated right. And to end his life over this wasn't right. It was a spur-of-the-moment kind of thing I couldn't fault or blame him for, but I wasn't going to stand idle.

As he struck, the knuckles of his right hand hitting my already bruised jaw with a loud crack and forcing my head to the side, I fought to stay on top of him. Pushing down all my weight, I tried to keep him pinned underneath me, a leg trapping him on either side. He hit again, and I couldn't shield my face, but I wasn't going to let the pain distract me.

"Listen to me, Tybalt," I pleaded, my voice raw and ragged with emotion. "You can't just throw your life away like this! If you're guilty, let the law decide your fate. Let them decide. But don't jump and end it like this."

He stilled underneath me, although I could tell he wasn't convinced by my words just yet.

"Please," I gasped, unaware that tears had started falling down my cheeks until I saw the droplets hit Tybalt's jacket, which I still clutched in my hands as I kept him pinned down. My shoulders shook, a wild trembling that was hard to subside, as I leaned over him, silently pleading for him to remain alive. I didn't want anyone else to die today.

"He could still be alive," I whispered again, tasting the bitter tang of blood. Tybalt must have hit me hard enough to cause damage, I thought, feeling the blood on my tongue.

His eyes met mine, dark and haunted as the night itself, and I could see the torment etched into every line and curve of his face.

"Even if he is alive," Tybalt replied

[236]

bitterly, "he'll never forgive me. And neither will I."

I watched him as he pursed his lips and turned his gaze away. "We've lost him."

"I refuse to believe that," I said, voice sharper than intended, but with a shock, I realized this was the case. I truly believed with all my heart that Mercutio was still alive. *He just had to be.*

"You could honor him by giving yourself to the police," I urged Tybalt to look at me, my grip on him tightening. *Whether Mercutio would be dead or alive after this.* "You could do this little thing for him. Live and face your guilt. For him."

His trembling hand reached up, and I flinched, fearing another hit. Instead, he gently caressed my cheek, brushing a stray strand of hair away from my eyes.

"I tried to step between you," he whispered hoarsely. "I nearly killed you. And yet… You're being kind." His voice broke. "You shouldn't forgive me either."

For a moment, we lay there, our breaths mingling in the chill air as the afternoon sun fell over us, tainting us in colors of orange and red. But then it happened. A sudden, sharp pain pierced through my chest, stealing the breath from my lungs. Tybalt's hand fell as I tried to scramble away from him. I doubled over, clutching at my shirt as if I could somehow tear

[237]

away the agony that threatened to consume me.

I choked, my eyes widening in horror as delicate petals spilled from my mouth and onto Tybalt's clothes. Panic flooded my vision, threatening to drown me in its merciless embrace.

"What the…?" Tybalt's anger melted away, replaced by genuine concern. He pushed himself up on his elbows and studied me. "What's wrong?"

I couldn't answer, couldn't even draw breath to speak as more petals tumbled from my lips. Tybalt moved so I wouldn't once again cover him with the petals. Instead, they fluttered to the ground like fragile butterflies, their beauty mocking me in my moment of weakness.

"What's happening?" Tybalt asked, his voice trembling as he sat next to me. I felt his hand come to rest on the small of my back, a comforting gesture made with long and unfamiliar sinewy fingers.

I still sat hunched. My arms crossed over my belly in an attempt to ease the pain that I felt in my stomach. But I kept heaving, finding it hard to catch a breath while the petals kept coming forth, taking away my breath and flow of oxygen.

I heard the concern in Tybalt's voice, "How long has this been going on?"

"Stay away," I managed to gasp, my

chest constricting with each labored breath. "Please."

"Damn it, Ben—" But Tybalt stopped himself, his features softening as he realized the severity of my condition. His gaze flicked between me and the petals, a silent understanding dawning in his eyes.

"Benvolio," he whispered, his voice barely audible above the gentle lap of the water. "Do you have any idea what's going on?"

"No," I choked out, as another wave of pain wracked my body, threatening to tear me apart from the inside out. I willed my body to ignore the pain, forcing myself to focus on Tybalt's concerned gaze. Drawing in a ragged breath, I struggled to speak through the strain of my choked voice.

"Ty... Tybalt," I managed to whisper, "this has been happening... for a while now."

"Since when?" he asked, trying to keep his composure while I could tell by the little tremble of his hand that he had to fight to keep calm. Whatever was happening to me, it seemed as if he knew more about it.

"Since... since that evening, when I spotted you and Mercutio together." A tear slid down my cheek because of the violent onset of coughs that followed, while Tybalt's eyes widened in shock as the truth set in.

And then another retch followed, and out

came a flower. An *entire* flower. It unfurled its delicate petals, each one a pale hue of pink tinged with hints of white. Its slender stem stood tall, crowned with a cluster of blossoms, each exuding a sweet, intoxicating fragrance that perfumed the air with a sense of freshness and renewal. As the gentle breeze danced through its petals, the flower seemed to shimmer with delicate grace.

My hand clawed at my chest as I sat hunched over, panting for breath, my eyes firmly fixed on the flower in front of me.

*An entire flower.*

That had never happened before. Petals, yes, in abundance. But an entire flower with the stem intact? The sight of it made my blood freeze, and had I not been trembling with the shocks of another cough, another petal or flower stuck in my throat, I might have sat frozen entirely.

"Benvolio, this isn't good," Tybalt's voice cracked, his face a mask of guilt and disbelief. I could hear him fumble, his hands idly searching for something. His phone?

I tried to look at him, but another tremor wrecked my body, and before I knew it, the motion had me stumble over. My body crumpled to the floor, wracked by violent coughs that tore more petals—and entire flowers now—from my throat. Their beauty mocked me, their colors an ironic contrast to the darkness within me. Pink. Fuchsia. *Mercutio.* The flowers reminded me of him.

"Stay with me, Ben," Tybalt urged, his hands shaking as he fumbled for his phone. The urgency in his movements betrayed his worry, though he tried to keep his voice steady. "I'm calling for help."

The world tilted, my vision blurring as if submerged in water, the edges of reality fraying into darkness. I tried to focus on Tybalt's face, but it danced away from me like a shadow on a wall.

"Stay with me, Benvolio," Tybalt murmured again, his hand warm against my back as he knelt beside me. A small comfort, yet one I clung to desperately. I could hear noises from the phone, but couldn't distinguish what was being said.

"Keep breathing, okay?" Tybalt's voice trembled. Everything after became a blur.

I think I saw the flashing light of another ambulance. I think I heard the footsteps of someone approaching as I was choking, my hands around my own neck as I tried to gasp for breath. But the flower was stuck there, cutting off my oxygen.

Black dots clouded my vision. They must have carried me into the ambulance because I faintly remember the orange-red hue of the sky

[241]

being replaced by the dull tones of white and gray.

As they loaded me into the ambulance, the last threads of consciousness slipped through my grasp like sand. The world went dark, and all that remained was an endless ocean of petals and flowers.

# Fifteen

The world flickered into existence, a bleached canvas of white. My eyelids fluttered—once, twice—and then I was squinting against the glare of merciless fluorescent lights looming above me. The air was heavy with that distinct, clinical scent. Sterile and indifferent.

A hospital.

My mind was racing, trying to piece together what had happened. Tybalt. The fight. Mercutio, lying in a pool of blood. *Oh God, Mercutio.* My heart clenched. *Is he...?*

Lying there, in a sea of crisp linens, everything came back to me like one awful flashback. My fingers twitched, longing for something real, something solid to hold and bring me back to a reality in which Mercutio was still there, smiling and vibrant. But all they grasped was emptiness, and so I clutched at the thin hospital blanket, grounding myself in its rough texture.

My thoughts were interrupted by the sound of footsteps. A doctor entered, his face grim. The sight of his solemn expression was enough to have my heart race wildly in my chest. What was going on? How long had I been out of it?

The doctor came to a halt at my bedside,

not even taking the effort to force a small smile.

"Mister Montague?" he asked.

"That's me," I confirmed. "Benvolio," I hesitated, surprised at the rawness of my own throat. Speaking hurt more than I had expected, and I found myself moving my jaw a few times without a sound coming out.

"Don't strain yourself," the doctor said, holding up a hand to shush me. I glared at him but quietly sank back against the thin pillow.

He remained silent for a moment, then spoke at a deliberately slow pace. "My name is Doctor Sampson. I'm afraid I have difficult news."

*No. Please no.* My hands gripped the bedsheets in dread. Was this about Mercutio? Had he not made it?

*It's silly, isn't it?* But in that moment, all my thoughts were focused on him, and not a single one was spared for me. I didn't think it was odd at the time. Mercutio had been stabbed. He'd been bleeding all over the pavement. So it was Mercutio whose life I feared for at that moment. I only realized my mistake when the doctor's eyes met mine, and he held up a file. Test results with my name on them.

"We had to extract entire flowers from you that were lodged down your windpipe."

I sat there, blinking, not quite understanding what the man said, until he turned around one of the papers he was holding. On it was a radiograph, an X-ray of my lungs. And in my lungs, I could see the weird, tangled vines with leaves.

But that was not possible, was it?

I looked up at the doctor, and all courage and hope drained from me. "What does that mean, doctor?" I asked, my voice strained, and each syllable felt like a knife cut the inside of my throat. What was this horror? Had it been caused by the flowers?

"You've been diagnosed with the Hanahaki disease."

A spiral of confusion tightened within me. The term was foreign, yet its cadence struck an ominous chord. As if I might have heard of it before, a long time ago. Apparently, my gaze was a question in itself as the doctor continued without me having to ask.

"Hanahaki is a very rare and life-threatening disease. It starts with a cough, possibly a chest ache, minor symptoms. Then petals will be coughed up, and eventually, entire flowers. As you can imagine, this brings risks. The petals or flowers can get stuck, blocking your windpipe, choking you."

I sat there, silently, and absorbed the information the best I could. Everything the doctor said sounded familiar. I'd been through all of that. I'd seen the flower before I passed

[245]

out.

"I understood from the young man who was found with you that you have been throwing up flowers for quite a while?" the doctor continued, his voice formal and monotonous. I could tell he felt little joy in telling me all this, which only caused the ominous feeling inside the pit of my stomach to grow.

I vaguely nodded. *I had a fucking plant inside of me.* That was all my mind registered. And it was growing too large.

"As the X-rays show, the disease has spread. At this point, the flowers come from your stomach, and the vines have nestled in your lungs." I had not thought it to be possible, but his expression grew even graver. His chin dipped, looking at me with intense eyes.

"I know you will have many questions, and I urge you to speak as little as possible, as your throat has sustained some light damage. We will provide you with a tablet to write on. For now, the most important thing to know is that Hanahaki is caused by unrequited love."

I froze as the doctor paused. Surely I had misheard him?

"Benvolio, do you know who has captured your heart?"

The doctor's words were clear and left no room for misinterpretation. Was my condition a result of unrequited love? Had I fallen for someone who did not feel the same way? The notion seemed absurd, and for a moment, I wondered if this was all an elaborate prank. I scanned the room, half-expecting a group of people to jump out and reveal that they had been recording the whole interaction as a joke. But no one appeared, no teenagers carrying phones or cameras. The doctor's face remained stern, his eyebrows furrowed in anticipation of my response. Was he truly waiting for me to answer?

I hesitated when I felt the rawness of my throat as if it were lined with thorns. Each swallow was a gruesome reminder of the pain that love had brought me. A love I had not dared to express. The love that made me cough up petals of pink, vivid fuchsia against my pale skin. The same shade as Mercutio's wild hair. *Of course, it's him. It's always been him.*

My dearest friend, my soulmate.

"I need a name, Mister Montague," the doctor urged, his expression still as stern. "Your life depends on it. If your crush returns the feelings, then you will be saved."

*Wait,* did the doctor mean that I would actually die because of this disease? *Stupid,* I thought. *Such a stupid way to die.*

"It's unfair," I managed to croak, but more words could not follow. My throat wouldn't allow me, and my chest tightened painfully.

Mercutio was my friend, but he did not love me in that way. And they were not going to force a fake confession out of him either. *It's unfair to ask someone's love,* I wanted to say. *Love should always be given willingly.* And for Mercutio's love, I would have been prepared to wait forever, even if it never came. *That is how love works.* You want the other to be happy, whether that is with or without you. If he had chosen Tybalt, I would have made my peace with it. He could have even chosen to be with Romeo or Rosaline, and I would have learned to live with it.

*So yes*, it was unfair that my life now depended on Mercutio. I didn't want him to be forced to choose me or anyone else. Because that's another thing about love. *Love takes time.*

It shouldn't be forced.

But instead of voicing my inner monologue, my lips parted in a silent sigh as I slumped back on the bed. The doctor misinterpreted what I wanted to say, letting out a low huff and filling in the void with words of his own while he ran a hand through his thinning hair.

"I agree. It isn't fair that you should suffer this. But the heart wants what the heart wants." The doctor shifted on his feet, staring

[248]

down at me. "So I will ask you once more, Mister Montague. Can you give me a name?"

"*Mercutio*," I didn't even stutter. His name escaped in a hushed exhale, filling the space between us with its weight. It was the first time I openly admitted it. These were feelings that I had pushed away, hidden safely like a treasure. Because they should have mattered to no one but me.

The doctor's frown deepened, etching lines of concern across his brow.

"Mercutio Escalus?" Recognition flickered in his eyes, and I nodded, a small, barely perceptible movement.

"Mercutio was brought in today after a street fight." His words filled the room, settling with a dull ache in my heart. "He is currently in the ICU."

A cold realization dawned on me. In the *intensive care unit.* Hurt. Vulnerable. *But alive?*

"Is he..." I couldn't finish the question, a combination of the disease and fear constricting my throat, choking the words before they could take flight. But the doctor silently lowered my files and then cleared his throat.

"This is unfortunate," he started, though he need not have bothered to say it. I could already tell by his whole posture that things were looking bad. "The wound Mercutio has sustained could have been vital. He is currently kept in a coma. He isn't in the clear yet."

His sentences were short and to the point, clear enough to leave no room for doubt. I stared ahead of me, solemnly, while I let the information sink in. Mercutio was here, still alive. He still had a chance. And so had I.

*If Mercutio were to wake up from the coma.*

If not… I turned my eyes back to the doctor, my fingers once again digging into the thin sheets of the bed. "If," the words pained me, not just physically but also emotionally. "If he doesn't waken…" *No, that wasn't right.* He had to wake up. I had to believe that he would. But I also didn't want the doctor to rush the process. Mercutio had to be stabilized enough to wake up. That much was clear.

"How long do we have?" I then asked instead. "How long do *I* have left?"

A shadow fell over the doctor's already grim expression, and I tightened my grip on the sheets until my knuckles turned white.

"Days at the most," his low voice grumbled.

*Days.* That was not what I wanted to hear. Would Mercutio recover enough to be awake in time? And even if he was, would he be conscious enough to listen? Would he understand what was going on? Should I even strain him like that by forcing this problem upon him?

[250]

*'Hi, you're awake after nearly dying. But hey, guess what? I need you to tell me that you love me, or I'll choke on a flower.'* That wasn't how I wanted him to wake up while he still had to recover.

"Days," the word left me like a breathless gasp, already committing to my fate. I knew the doctor had said I should speak as little as possible, but I couldn't care less right now.

"We have already informed your parents and your sister," the doctor said, and for the first time since his arrival, I saw a little spark of compassion in his eyes. It was as if his expression softened, and his shoulders became less tense. He took up the files again, holding them against his chest.

"We may have another option," he continued, a hesitant thread of hope weaving through his professional demeanor. The papers rustled as he shifted them, the sound oddly soothing in the stark silence of the hospital room. I lifted my gaze to meet his, finding something new kindled there, a glimmer that wasn't present before.

He cleared his throat. "There's a specialist in Japan. She's been working on an experimental treatment for the Hanahaki disease. It's a surgical procedure that," he paused, assessing my reaction before continuing. "That could potentially remove the flowers without... without necessitating the reciprocation

[251]

of feelings."

I felt a surge within me, like a ray of hope. This might be the lifeline I was so desperate for, yet with it came a torrent of new fears and uncertainties.

"But?" I prompted, my voice barely above a whisper, every word scratching my throat like thorns.

"But," he echoed, drawing out the word as if it weighed heavily on his tongue. "She would have to come from Japan, and given the current circumstances, it could take a few days to arrange her arrival. Possibly longer."

*Days that I might not have.* I closed my eyes, feeling the dread that had momentarily lifted settle back upon my shoulders. Time was a luxury I wasn't sure I had. My chest felt tighter, constricted by the very petals that threatened to choke me. I opened my eyes slowly, meeting the doctor's gaze with an intensity born of desperation.

"Days?" The question sounded more like a plea, but I needed him to understand. I didn't know if I, or Mercutio, had that much time.

The doctor nodded solemnly, the softness in his eyes replaced by the hard edge of reality once again. "I'm afraid so. And even then, there's no guarantee of success. The procedure is still in its experimental stages."

My heart sank at his words. It was as if

the doctor had seen my expression, for he spoke up again, voice kinder.

"I will contact her and see if we can get her over as quickly as possible. But for now... Would you like to see Mercutio?" The doctor's question came unexpectedly, and I realized he was making an exception for me to see Mercutio. *A chance I could not waste.*

"Yes," I said, my voice steadier than I felt. "Yes, I do."

The doctor gave a slight nod, understanding perhaps more than he let on. He moved around the side of my bed, calling out discreetly for a nurse to come and give a helping hand. With a practiced motion, he produced a wheelchair from seemingly nowhere. It must have been tucked away in a corner I hadn't noticed. He unfolded it with an efficient flick, its steel arms expanding with mechanical precision. Then he looked at me, and it clicked in my mind. He wanted me to sit in... that?

"We can't have you walk in your condition," he said, possibly an answer to the silent raise of my brow. I'd been walking just fine only hours or so ago, and now I was told I had to sit in a wheelchair. It was unexpected, weird. It made everything seem more real somehow, harder to deny.

"We want to minimize any strain on your body. Any movement could trigger a coughing fit, which could be life-threatening," the doctor explained as he motioned toward the wheelchair. I hesitated but understood and let them assist me into the chair.

I was wheeled down the sterile, labyrinthine corridors, the antiseptic scent mingling with my own fear. Lights hummed softly overhead, casting a pallid glow that felt otherworldly as it reflected off the bleach-white walls. I could see nurses and other doctors moving briskly, their shoes whispering secrets against the polished floor that I couldn't decipher.

The door to Mercutio's room swooshed open at our approach, and time seemed to slow. I braced myself for what lay within, but when my eyes met his still form on the hospital bed, nothing could've prepared me for the hollowness that carved itself in my chest.

There he was. Pale. Silent. How delicate he appeared, tethered to life by tubes and wires. It was the very antithesis of him. Mercutio danced on the edge of recklessness and laughed in the face of danger with a glint in his deep brown eyes that could outshine the stars. A pang of longing twisted inside me, a yearning so strong it bordered on agony, knowing that this might be the last time I could see him. I swallowed down the petals that threatened to come forth, very aware of Doctor Sampson's

[254]

scrutinizing gaze.

Carefully, I lifted my hand, fingers trembling. I placed them on top of Mercutio's, ignoring the cold of the tape and the tubes and only focusing on the softness of his skin. He felt too cold, not warm enough. But he was still alive, and for that, I should be grateful.

I forced a small smile, studying him as he lay there. Mercutio's fuchsia hair spread across the pillow like a vibrant halo. Someone had tried to tame the wild flames of that hair, combing it gently to the side in an attempt to bring some normalcy to his extraordinary nature.

They did not know that Mercutio was anything but ordinary.

A ray of evening sunlight slipped through the blinds and played upon his features, casting shadows that seemed to accentuate the angular structure of his cheekbones and the gentle slope of his nose. His eyelashes were dark against his skin, long and absurdly perfect with a wayward curl that instilled in me a desire to touch them gently, reassuring myself he was indeed there, that I had not dreamed him up.

I held his hand, wishing that he would notice me. That I was here with him.

"Mercutio," my voice sounded horrible, croaked and dry. Yet I hoped that he recognized me. That he was aware.

Tears gathered like unwelcome guests at

[255]

the corners of my eyes, blurring my vision until I blinked them away. The sight of him, motionless and vulnerable, tore through my carefully maintained armor. I squeezed his hand, a feeble attempt to infuse some of my own strength into him, to will him into waking.

I leaned forward, my forehead nearly touching his as I whispered his name again. This time, it was a plea, a prayer sent out into the void of sterile smells and quiet beeps. "Mercutio…"

The silence enveloped us, a sacred stillness punctuated only by the steady rhythm of his heart monitor.

"Mercutio," I began again, voice barely audible above the hum of life-saving machinery, "you infuriate me. Always being so reckless. Yet… With every ridiculous stunt you pull, every boundary you cross with that impish grin on your face... You draw me into your orbit." My fingertips traced the line of his jaw, reverently soft. "I find myself caught in your wake, always by your side, never wanting to be anywhere else."

I took a shaky breath, knowing the doctor and the nurses were still there. I knew the noises of their shoes, the instruments with which they worked, and the voices of other patients they were helping, might drown out my voice. But I had to say it. If not now, then perhaps I'd never get the chance again.

"I love you, Mercutio."

*Did he hear me?*

There was no sign of it. But still, I hoped.

# Sixteen

The steady beep of the heart monitor filled the hospital room. I lay motionless in the bed, exhausted from another coughing fit that left my throat raw and aching. A nurse was by my side. She had introduced herself to me as 'Joy', although I heavily suspected her real name was 'Emanuela' since it was what Sampson called her. The two seemed to have a thing going on that they discreetly tried to hide from my eyes.

Joy bustled about, fluffing my pillow with a forced cheeriness when the door creaked open, and a familiar face peeked in.

"Special delivery for Mister Benvolio!" Romeo cried in a sing-song voice. He sauntered to my bedside with his acoustic guitar slung over his shoulder. Nurse Joy looked up in surprise, and he flashed her a charming smile. *Always the charlatan.* I could see the blush creep onto her cheeks, and I subdued the urge to roll my eyes. *Romeo was at it again.*

"Well, beautiful ladies," here Romeo paused after winking at Joy, and then he turned his attention back to me, making me jump slightly. "And beautiful sirs."

"Romeo, what in the world," I started, but the words died on my lips as he took the guitar from his shoulder and started to play, filling the room with a melody that was as clumsy as it was earnest.

"O Benvolio, you lie in repose. Your cheeks lack their usual rose," Romeo sang, and I frowned. I didn't blame Joy for silently leaving the room. *Just to make it clear*, Romeo's voice wasn't unpleasant. It was actually smooth and gentle most of the time, enough to lure in any beauty, pleasant enough that I usually enjoyed listening to him. It was just the fact that he was singing off-key that made it difficult to take him seriously right now.

*I silently hoped he had never serenaded any of his crushes.*

"But fear not, cousin, for I am here," Romeo continued. "To serenade away your every fear!"

*No, no matter how hard I tried not to laugh, I couldn't help it.* I couldn't help but chuckle despite the tightness in my chest and the absurdity of it all. Only Romeo could find humor at a time like this, and I found myself grateful for his ridiculous antics.

"Ah, but this is no ordinary tune," he declared, pausing dramatically before launching into a ballad that was surprisingly more melodic. "This, dear cousin, is the song of my heart."

His fingers danced across the strings, conjuring up a sweet, melancholic sound that resonated within the hollow spaces of the room. I listened, entranced by how Romeo was finally playing something in tune.

"From Verona's streets to this quiet room, my love for you dispels all gloom. I could have had girls by the dozen, but none compare to you, dear cousin."

A lump formed in my throat at his words. I knew what he was trying to do. Bringing me a love song in a typical Romeo kind of way. It was a declaration, not of romantic love, but of something deeper. We were family and best friends. And why shouldn't those types of love, in so many cases stronger than the romantic kind that sometimes shows to be fleeting and temporary, work? It was a valid attempt.

"Thank you, Romeo," I whispered, my voice barely audible over the dwindling chords.

"It's love you need, so let me be clear, I love no one like I love you," Romeo added as the music died and his voice started to strain. I couldn't withhold another laugh when I saw the worried expression on his face, the way his brow drew up while he was visibly racking his brain for a word that could rhyme with 'clear'. And when he got it, his smile grew into his dazzling toothpaste one.

"My *dear*," he finished, clearly proud of the ending he had invented for his song.

"Really?" I waited a beat as I watched him intently, seeing him grow more insecure with every passing second. "Must you serenade me on my deathbed?" I rasped, but a hint of a smile tugged at my lips.

"Chin up, cousin! This one's guaranteed to lift your spirits." Romeo strummed a dramatic chord. "Ode to My Dearest Benvolio," he began, his voice wavering with emotion.

He leaped up and fell to one knee beside me. "My love for you is boundless as the sea, eternal as the stars!" he declared. "Marry me, Benvolio, and I will cherish you forever!"

Now, we were both laughing despite the pain in my chest and the coughs that interfered. Once we calmed down, I gently smiled at him. "You're too kind, cousin. But I'm afraid your love cannot cure me."

Romeo's face fell. He set down his guitar and perched on the edge of the bed. "I know. But we'll find a way," he said softly, eyes brimming with sudden tears. "I can't lose you."

The light from the window cast a warm, golden hue across Romeo's face, softening the stark lines of worry that had taken residence there.

"Don't fret. You haven't lost me yet," I whispered. The words felt fragile on my tongue, delicate, and easily crushed. I wanted to believe them, to wrap myself in the comfort they

[261]

offered, but deep within my chest, there was an ache that told another story.

Romeo reached for my hand, his grip firm and warm.

"We're Montagues," he said with a hint of a smile that didn't quite reach his eyes. "We stick together through everything."

I hummed, my throat too painful to agree vocally. I glanced at the tablet on my bedside table but didn't want to use it.

"I don't understand why this should not work." Romeo's expression crumpled into a pout, his exuberance fading. "I do love you, truly. And isn't the love between family the greatest of all? Why should it not work?"

I smiled weakly, a twinge in my chest making me wince. "Romantic love…" I started, but he cut me off.

"I know. It has to be romantic love. I just think it is bullshit," he muttered, his hand leaving my own so he could brush the hair from my damp forehead. The sound of a hesitant shuffle at the doorway stilled him. Standing in the doorway, I saw Rosaline and Livia Capulet framed against the white threshold, looking as if they had stepped out of one of Livia's surreal sketches.

Both girls seemed to be fidgeting with their hands, Livia holding a card between them, which appeared to be something she had drawn herself. Rosaline was holding a 'get well soon' baby blue balloon. I had to smile at the sight of them.

"I like it," I rasped, pointing weakly at the balloon Rosaline was carrying.

She looked up at it, then quickly glanced at me again and grinned. "You have no idea how much trouble it cost me to get one. A Capulet buying a blue balloon?"

*Ah, the family-feud thing.* I wondered if her parents had been with her when she had walked into the shop to buy one. If they had, they would have died a thousand deaths. Their daughter, buying a blue balloon. *Imagine!* I grinned at the thought.

Romeo patted the bed while the girls walked over to my bedside. Livia instantly showed me her postcard, holding it close enough to my face to make the drawing seem like one blurry mess.

"Not so close," her sister berated her, and she held it at a further distance so I could see. The colorful drawing depicted a pleasant lakeside view with me standing in front of it, smiling. I raised a brow at her, and she let out a shy little laugh.

"What?" she said. "I'd already started this one for my collection. But thought it might be nicer if I gave it to you."

There were two disturbing revelations in

there. One, she had been drawing me. And two, she had wanted to keep that drawing herself. I raised a brow but decided not to comment on these two little details.

"Because I like to look at myself?" I asked instead, sarcastically, accepting the card with a weak movement of my hand. Weak, because I lacked the strength, not because I didn't admire the gesture.

Livia laughed, loudly now, holding her sleeve up in front of her lips. "I know you like to look at pretty sights."

Once again, I subdued the need to roll my eyes. "Yes, *pretty sights*," I repeated. "Pretty *views*. That lake, for instance, is gorgeous."

"What my cousin is trying to say," Romeo interjected on my behalf, his arm spread out in front of my face to shut me up, and I glared accusingly at him. "Is that he is delighted to accept this beautiful drawing from you, Livia."

"No," I grumbled, "I don't like the look of me in this at all—"

"As I said, he is thrilled," Romeo pushed me down on the bed with one strong arm, and I grumbled into his back, my fingers twitching in the air.

*Fine,* I thought, feeling like I had no other option but to give in and surrender. *Delighted I was then.*

[264]

Romeo smirked down at me, and I gratefully took a deep breath once his arm left my chest. I tried to sit up again when Livia stepped forward, the harsh hospital lights casting shadows across her freckled face, giving her an ethereal glow.

"I have something to say," she announced, her voice clear and surprisingly steady despite the tremors I could see coursing through her fingers.

Rosaline's eyes widened marginally, a silent acknowledgment of her sister's rare courage. Romeo glanced between us, a silent understanding passing between us that he should give space for what was about to unfold. He slowly slid from the bed, making sure that Livia could come to stand right by my side.

I felt betrayed, a little, by him. Because now I was completely at her mercy, delivered to her roving eyes as she looked down at me so seriously. It was downright creepy.

"Uh, Romeo?" I tried, but my voice creaked, and none of the letters came out recognizable.

"Please," Livia said, taking a deep breath as she tried to ground herself, clearly as nervous as I was. "Don't tire yourself, Ben. I'll only take a moment."

Now, that scared me even more. My eyes searched for Romeo's, silently pleading with him

[265]

to come and save me from whatever confession Livia was about to make. I even searched for Rosaline, but she had moved away from my bed and out of my sight completely.

*What if Livia was going to tell me she still loved me?*

"I know Hanahaki was caused by unrequited love, but," here Livia worried her bottom lip, and I felt a sinking feeling in the pit of my stomach. *Here we go,* I thought.

"I know how you feel. I was there only a few weeks ago. Pining after you."

*I knew it.* I squeezed my eyes shut for the tiniest moment, giving myself a small reprieve from the love confession she was bound to force upon me once more.

"And then I found someone else," Livia continued, and I opened my eyes.

*Wait. What?*

"Which is why," Livia said, eyes all bright and sparkly and smile wide and cheerful. She spread her arms open wide, a grand gesture, while behind her, Rosaline and Juliet appeared holding a large A3 paper with photos and pictures glued onto it. "We have prepared some alternatives for you. We're gonna save your life, Ben," she finished with a wink.

And I was left speechless.

Juliet and Rosaline held the paper up in front of me, allowing me the chance to cast my eyes over the innumerable pictures of men. Well, mostly men. I recognized a girl or two between them and raised a brow.

"That one's Trans," Juliet pointed out to me, as if she had been reading my mind. Then she pointed at another lady. "And this one we added because she's just absolutely gorgeous."

I looked up at her flushed face and saw the excitement in her eyes. Then I glanced at Rosaline and Livia, who stood on the other side, nodding excitedly. Even Romeo, who had taken a few steps back, was smiling a hopeful smile.

"You guys," I said, my words stuttering. This was the *sweetest thing* and completely unexpected. The paper was filled with pictures cut from newspapers and magazines, some printed from the internet. Had the girls really gone through all the trouble to make me this?

"We thought you could hang it above your bed," Livia said cheerily.

Now, that was an embarrassing thought, but *oh-so sweet*. And I could tell they had put in the effort. I gently traced the edges of the collage, feeling the ridges where different textures met, a blend of glossy magazine cutouts and the grainy finish of inkjet prints. There was a variety of faces staring back at me, diverse in their beauty and allure. Some had sharp, striking features, while others boasted warm, inviting smiles. I found myself lingering on a picture I

[267]

wished I hadn't seen, one that made my heart inexplicably skip.

A model that bore an uncanny resemblance to Mercutio.

There was the colored hair, not pink but something colorful all the same. Like he had jumped out of a rainbow. The model's eyes, though not as dark or deep as Mercutio's, held a similar mischievous spark. He even wore a blue silk shirt that mirrored Mercutio's vivid taste in clothing.

My chest tightened with a sense of yearning so acute it bordered on pain. A familiar tickle began in my throat. I knew it the moment it started. This was going to be bad.

My hand clasped over my mouth as if I could physically hold back the onslaught of what was to come. Coughs wracked my body in violent spasms, each contraction squeezing the air from my lungs and drawing curious gazes from my friends. I could see the concern in their eyes, heard it in the echoes of their voices as they called my name.

"Benvolio? Are you all right?" Romeo's voice had lost its earlier cheerfulness.

The tickle intensified, a prickling sensation as if a thousand tiny petals were caught in my airways. I tried to suppress it, fearing the roughness of entire flowers forcing their way up my throat. Fearing the loss of

[268]

breath.

The girls' excitement morphed into concern, their brows furrowing. Livia moved swiftly, folding the poster with practiced hands, pulling it away just in time for the first petals to flow.

Petals piled upon the bedding, creating a little pyramid of pink while I reached for my neck and gasped for breath.

"This doesn't look good," I heard someone—was it Rosaline?—say. And was that blood on the blanket?

"Call for help," was that still her or someone else?

"Push the button!"

I vaguely registered how my friends were moving around me, how one of them must have found the emergency button and pressed it, how the door opened, and a nurse came rushing in to help.

I was put upright in the bed and felt hands upon me. Someone tried the Heimlich, which worked only briefly, as an entire flower fell from my lips. But then, another was already climbing its way up my throat. There were rushed voices all around me, but my vision had started to blur, and the lack of oxygen was taking away all of my senses. Another firm jostle, another flower that tumbled from my lips. I had lost count.

But I knew one thing for certain: my time was up.

All I knew at that moment was that I was losing this battle. That more and more flowers, in full bloom, were making their way toward my lips. This was exactly what the doctor had warned me would happen, and if it did, it could be fatal.

Just then, a familiar voice drowned out all others as Nurse Joy came bursting in, frantic energy propelling her to my bedside.

"It's Mercutio," she said, loud enough near my ear to hear. And perhaps I would have heard her anyway, for the name of Mercutio was enough to capture my attention even in the throes of death. And then she brought the news everyone was hoping for.

"He's awake."

As another flower blocked my throat, making me choke and sputter for air, I could only think of him… *Mercutio was awake?*

"Mercutio is awake, and he demands to see you. So don't die on us now, Benvolio," I heard Joy's distinctive voice.

*I wasn't planning on it*, but the flowers seemed to have a different idea.

As I teetered on the brink of life and death, I heard a voice that brought me back fully.

A familiar voice calling my name.

[270]

# Seventeen

**M**y only thought was of Mercutio. Wild, energetic Mercutio with his fuchsia hair and electric smile. *How my secret love for him has become my undoing.*

"Out of my way!" The sudden clamor shattered the quietude, and my heart lurched in my chest. *It was him. Mercutio.*

Surely, I was dreaming?

I heard him at first, but when I forced my eyes open, I could see that he had entered the room in a flurry of nurses, the steady hand of Doctor Sampson guiding his wheelchair. His face was taut with fear, those deep brown eyes that so often sparkled with mischief were now pools of dread.

*Was I truly awake?*

"Ben... Ben!" he rasped. That he could even sit in the wheelchair seemed like a miracle to me. His voice was filled with urgency and something akin to terror. But he was here, despite his wounds—a crimson stain seeping through the bandages on his chest, a stark reminder of the violence that brought us here.

Our eyes locked, and for a moment, I saw the unbridled spirit that refused to be caged by circumstance or injury. Mercutio's presence ignited a flicker of hope within me, even as

[271]

another petal escaped, dancing its way down onto the cold floor.

*Please,* I wanted to say, *don't look at me with such despair.* But the words were trapped behind the relentless tide of blossoms I could not stop.

*Please,* another thought. *I love you.*

Doctor Sampson moved to intervene, but Mercutio waved him off, his focus never leaving my face. There was an unspoken conversation in our gaze, layers of emotion that we danced around, hidden beneath jokes and playful banter. Now, in the sterile light of the hospital, under the shadow of mortality, everything unsaid was heavy between us. Surfacing.

"Stay with me, Benvolio," he whispered, the tremble in his voice betraying the bravado he usually wore like armor. And though I was drowning in a sea of petals, his plea was a lifeline I desperately grasped.

The world around us faded. Our hands met, his fingers wrapping around mine. His touch, normally charged with electric vivacity, was now a gentle whisper against my clammy skin, soothing, grounding.

"You can't die like this, Benvolio. Not choking on flowers," Mercutio's voice broke through the fog of my pain, urgent yet imbued with a gentleness I've seldom seen from him. His face was a blur, but the desperation in his dark

[272]

eyes pierced through the haze.

And then he said it. The words I had longed to hear but never dared to hope for.

*"I love you."*

This was not the way either of us had envisioned this happening. It should have been a confession in romantic moonlight instead of underneath the harsh, unforgiving fluorescence of the hospital lights.

I felt the soft squeeze of his hand. But other than that, nothing happened. I don't know why I had expected some kind of magic, for the petals inside my chest to dwindle and disappear upon the confession. But that didn't happen. The flower stuck between my lips proved this wasn't over yet.

*Was this normal?* Anchored by Mercutio's touch, by him holding my hand as firmly as he could with his injuries, I started to panic, my eyes scouring the room to see how the girls and Romeo stood huddled together at the far end. The nurses had all surrounded our bed, Doctor Sampson standing at the end. Then my eyes went back to Mercutio. *Always Mercutio.* Even in his hospital garb, he looked so wonderful, so alive, like a spirit of dreams.

And I could see how Mercutio's eyes turned wide as I coughed up new petals.

"You idiot, to let it come this far," his voice broke through the fog of my despair, the

[273]

familiar lilt of affection mingled with a raw edge of fear. I felt his fist on my back, not too hard. It reminded me of all the times we had playfully wrestled. He was trying to get the petals out, to stop me from choking.

"Don't die," he said, his voice raw and wrecked with emotion. "Don't you dare die on me now, Benvolio. I do not plan to be dating my own hand for the rest of my life, you hear me?"

I reached out for Mercutio, my fingers trembling and my grip weak. Even now, he still joked. *Typical.*

I tried to speak. But petals made me choke the first time, and then the second. By my third attempt, I was heaving and my throat felt raw.

"You've got a lovely hand," I said, forcing a smile despite the soreness of my lips.

"Joker," Mercutio murmured, but I saw the affection in his eyes. "That's my role. I make the jokes here."

"Mercutio... I... I love you," the words crawled from my lips, each syllable heavy with emotion. Petals fluttered to the ground as I spoke. My chest heaved with the effort of each breath.

"Finally," Mercutio whispered. And then he moved forward unexpectedly. I could hear the collective intake of breaths from those around us as Mercutio pressed his lips against mine, and then I was lost in the feeling of him.

His kiss was an unexpected warmth, a gentle pressure that was at once grounding and elevating. It stole the breath I struggled to reclaim, yet gave me a new life altogether.

The harsh lights overhead dimmed as my world narrowed to the touch of Mercutio's lips on mine, soft and forgiving. A whisper of fuchsia tickled my senses, and the electric tingle that danced across my skin seemed to tease out the lightness within my chest.

I could breathe again.

I felt light. Lighter than ever before.

And as he broke the kiss, the intensity of his gaze burned into me, binding me to the spot. His hands were now on my shoulders, as if he could hold the very soul within me together with the force of his touch. The raw honesty of his eyes, those deep wells of brown that I could fall into without a second thought, told me that he understood everything.

And I suddenly understood that the unsaid things between us had always been louder than words. Why had we needed to voice it? It had been clear, evident. I loved him. He loved me.

Around us, the sterile room echoed with the beeps and hums of medical machinery. But Mercutio drew all my focus. I searched his eyes. The fuchsia strands of his hair fell across his

[275]

brow, a vibrant contrast to the sterile white of the hospital walls. His own breaths matched mine. Then, something shifted in his expression. The corner of his mouth quirked up.

"Benvolio," he whispered, almost reverently, and I felt his fingers dig into my skin. Hot, warm, *alive*.

"Has anyone ever told you that you're a pretty boy?"

Did he really just say that in front of all the hospital staff and our friends?

"Yeah," I murmured, my throat still sore. But no new petals seemed to rise, for which I was grateful. I let my fingers slip down Mercutio's bandaged skin, his side, careful not to trace past the wound, as I did not want to accidentally hurt him. "You did."

"So I did," Mercutio said, grinning weakly. "Many a time. And you never thought to take it seriously?"

"Huh?" *Way to go, Benvolio! Great conversation.* I blinked at him.

"Yeah, huh," Mercutio replied with a grin as wide as he could muster at the moment. His fuchsia hair flopped in front of his eyes, and he had to lift one hand to brush it away. I instantly regretted the loss of his warmth.

"You can't blame a guy for assuming you were just being your usual flirty self," I retorted softly, trying to ignore how my hand yearned to

[276]

reach out to him once more.

"Pfft," Mercutio scoffed, though the sparkle in his eyes softened the sound. "Benvolio Montague, are you calling me a flirt?"

"Well, it seems Benvolio is cured," I heard Doctor Sampson's voice somewhere behind us. The cheers of the others watching us took me by surprise. Mercutio's laugh, normally a boisterous sound that filled the room, was now a mere whisper of what it used to be. It still managed to light up his eyes with that familiar mischievous sparkle.

"Benny, I'm hurt." He feigned shock, one hand pressed against his heart as if wounded by my words. "I've been pouring my soul out, and here you are calling it mere flirtation."

I couldn't help the smile that tugged at the corners of my mouth. Even with bandages wrapping his torso like an unwanted shawl, Mercutio had the power to make the world seem less heavy.

"You're incorrigible," I said, voice filled with a mix of exasperation and affection. My gaze wandered over his features, from the delicate arch of his brow to the unyielding intensity in his brown eyes.

"But you love me for it," he said, his voice dancing with lightness and playful banter.

"Yes, I love you for it," I replied, a coy smile tugging at the corners of my lips. I loved every bit of Mercutio, *especially* his mischievous side. But I wasn't going to let him know that.

"We need to do another check, Mister Montague," the doctor interrupted our conversation, giving me a knowing but also relieved look. "I'm going to arrange for another scan to be made, see if that chest of yours is indeed cured, though I have little doubt." He clicked his tongue. "Procedures."

I nodded to show I understood and watched as Doctor Sampson turned and left the room. Then I faced Mercutio with a smile. He was already laughing with Romeo and the others, skin pale and chest bandaged. But he was looking more and more like himself again.

Watching him like this made me wonder... If we had always been in love with each other, then why had I fallen ill? What had triggered the disease?

A memory surfaced.

*Oh, it must have been that.*

As if Mercutio sensed my worried thoughts, he looked at me and sighed. "I can hear you worrying again, Benvolio. You have no right to. I just cured you."

I shrugged, relieved to feel I could make that motion again, even if my muscles felt stiff after all the coughing from the past few days.

"I told you, I am an excellent nurse," Mercutio said with a wink.

[278]

"Among other things," I mocked, as his words took me back to when he helped me escape from Livia and walked me home. "I still haven't found out what other things you meant."

Mercutio merely looked at me with a smirk. "Imagine the joy of finding out," he mused. "Besides," his voice turned more serious now, "had I known you felt this way about me, I'd have told you much sooner."

*Wait...*"What?" was the only sensible word that came from my lips.

"Oh yeah," Mercutio continued unperturbed. "For some reason, I always thought you were into girls. And then you grew so close to Livia, and I just assumed..." his voice trailed off while he made gestures with his hands. "Anyway, I was so relieved when you told me you weren't interested in her and I... I don't know, Ben. I should have taken my chances just right then. I waited too long."

I hesitated. Had I heard him correctly? "No," I gasped, fully aware that our friends had gathered around us, keenly watching and listening. "No, it was my fault. I thought you were dating Tybalt in secret."

Mercutio's whisper of a laugh rumbled through the room. "You idiot," he grumbled, rubbing a hand past his face as he regained his composure.

[279]

"Listen and listen closely, Benvolio," Mercutio said, his voice low and stern. "I might have made you believe that a little longer because I wanted to make you jealous. Okay? I mean, you had Livia, Romeo had Juliet—"

"He had not," Juliet's voice came from behind us, annoyed.

"Or Rosaline or Suzy or whoever," Mercutio waved the words away with a roll of his eyes as if to say, 'who was still keeping track?'

"But the kiss," I murmured.

"It was nothing more than curiosity."

And I was inclined to believe him because Mercutio had a long history of dating and kissing numerous people. What was one Capulet among all of his conquests? *Except for a mistake?*

A knowing smirk played across my lips as I quipped, "You know what they say. Curiosity killed the cat."

Mercutio's eyes narrowed with mischief. "Well, now that you mention it… How is our dear Prince of Cats?"

"Tybalt?" I asked, stammering foolishly because up until now, I hadn't even spared the fate of the Capulet a single thought. My mind had been solely focused on Mercutio, on his wounds and his recovery. *On our love.* What had happened to Tybalt after I fell at his feet?

The affirmative melody of Mercutio's hum filled the air, a light and carefree tune that seemed to dance on the breeze.

"My cousin is alive and well," Rosaline's voice sounded, making me turn my head to look at her. Her eyes were sparkling with knowledge as she stepped closer to us.

"He turned himself in right after calling an ambulance for Benvolio," she announced, and I watched how Mercutio's gaze became thoughtful.

"Huh?" he said, and I realized he probably hadn't heard how I'd gotten in here.

"Yeah, it was Tybalt who called the alarm when Benvolio started to choke," Romeo interjected, joining Rosaline's side. "Without him, Benvolio would have been dead."

A scowl slid over Mercutio's face as if he had difficulty accepting that fact. But then he seemed to recompose himself, although his expression remained sour. "So that rat-catcher did something good for once," he said with a grimace. "Because he surely isn't a good kisser. Ugh!"

Loud cries echoed throughout the room as my friends pulled horrified faces, and Romeo cried out, "Too much information, Mercutio!" Which left me chuckling because the sight was funny.

The few nurses who were still in the

[281]

room stood bewildered before quickly exiting. Only Nurse Joy remained, a small smile playing on her lips as she observed us.

"Well," Mercutio started while he tried to run a hand through his hair, the movement was slowed down by his injuries, though. "I suppose I should thank him then. Do they accept flowers in jail?"

Now, it was Rosaline's turn to let out a laugh. She nearly doubled over, and Juliet came to stand behind her to pat her back comfortingly.

"He's not in jail," Rosaline said, biting back more giggles. "We paid his bail."

"You did what?" Mercutio nearly shouted, making me flinch. He seemed to have caught sight of it, for he reached for my ears, covering them with his hands, before he repeated his words, but softer. *"What did you just say?"*

"He's not in jail," Livia answered instead of her sister.

"Whyever not?" Mercutio cried out, his hands still nice and warm on my ears. "Need I remind you, he nearly *killed* me?"

"Yes, well. But he's, like, super bummed about it," Livia started, and I had to stifle another laugh because it was such an insensitive way to say that Tybalt felt sorry about what he had done. It looked like Mercutio wasn't ready yet to let the topic go, but Doctor Sampson came

[282]

into the room and shushed everyone.

"I understand that this is one joyful reunion," he started. Mercutio's hands fell from my ears, but the warmth lingered as if his touch had kindled a small flame within me. "But we mustn't forget that our patients here are still on the mend," the doctor continued. "It seems young Mister Escalus will have to be returned to his bed to rest."

Doctor Sampson then turned to me, his expression a blend of professional satisfaction and human empathy. "And you, young Montague… You have an appointment with the X-ray this afternoon. Your parents have been informed. And you'll have a sore throat for some time," he warned, "but the worst is over."

Nurse Joy smiled. "You've been through quite the ordeal," she commented, her gaze soft upon me before scanning the room. "All of you have."

Then she turned back to me. "You're on the mend, Benvolio," she said, her voice the melody of a lullaby. "Mercutio's love has cured you."

A slow smile stretched across Mercutio's lips. "Hear that?" he said, sounding a bit too enthusiastic. "I am a doctor too now."

"Yeah, yeah, I know," I fake grumbled. "First, you were a nurse, now you're promoted to love doctor."

[283]

The sound of laughter filled the room. *We were going to be okay.*

"Curing one patient doesn't make you a doctor, though," Joy said once the laughter faded.

Mercutio pursed his lips, frowning. "Doesn't it?" That silly look on his face made me laugh again, and I wasn't the only one. Nurse Joy's laughter filled the room, bright and infectious.

"But isn't it odd," Livia began, her words directed at Joy, "that Benvolio could fall this ill when Mercutio loved him all along? It doesn't make sense. Why didn't I fall ill when my love was unrequited?"

"Yes," Juliet piped in. "That's a good question." *And I thought so too.*

"If people had Hanahaki every time their love went unanswered," Rosaline said and then eyed Romeo, who stood a few paces to her left. "Well...Romeo would have been dead a thousand times over."

"Hey!" Romeo shouted, insulted, then blushed because he knew she was right. Juliet eyed him with a smirk, but she didn't apologize.

"True love," Joy whispered, then glanced at Doctor Sampson from the corners of her eyes—a gaze that conveyed more than words could. "Will you explain this to them?" she asked him.

[284]

"Well," the doctor said, thoughtfully tapping his finger against his arm. "Hanahaki is a rare disease, uncommon. Love is an everyday occurrence, and if all it took was for such love to remain unanswered, then the disease would not have been rare but common. Love remains unanswered most of the time," he started explaining, and we all leaned in a little closer to hear what he was about to say.

"Hanahaki only festers when true love is involved. We haven't cracked the why of it. We only know it hardly ever occurs. So be assured, having a crush on someone won't kill you. Usually."

Romeo let out a sigh of relief. I felt Mercutio gently squeeze my hand.

"Don't be scared to fall in love and to be rejected," Doctor Sampson continued, his eyes sliding past all of us, one by one. "True love sounds wonderful, and people think it is rare. That it hardly exists. In reality, true love is everywhere. It feels special, and it is, but it isn't unique. There will always be someone else you can fall in love with and who might love you in turn. Love should make both parties happy. If your love isn't reciprocated, then let it be. Don't hunt it down, don't chase it, don't force it. Love should come naturally. If one of the two isn't willing to love the other fully, neither will truly become happy. Love has to happen both ways.

[285]

And here, in the case of Benvolio and Mercutio, it was a love so true and so pure… Like I said. One in a billion chance."

"You hear that?" Mercutio said, a goofy smile plastered on his face. "What we have is special."

"You need a doctor to tell you that?" I asked, raising a brow teasingly. He removed his hand from my grip, only to give me a playful slap against my chest.

"Sounds like they're both doing much better to me, doctor," Rosaline said with a smirk.

Doctor Sampson rolled his eyes and took a few steps from my bed. "Now, I need to be about my day," he stated firmly.

"Oh, before you go," the words tumbled from my lips without thinking. "Could Mercutio perhaps be placed in my room?"

The doctor considered this for a moment. "Well, since he is awake and his life is no longer in imminent danger, I suppose that can be arranged."

Relief flooded over me at the idea of having my friend close by during my recovery. I couldn't help but smile broadly at the thought.

"Thank you, doctor," I said gratefully. He nodded in acknowledgment before he turned and left the room, leaving us with Nurse Joy. I heard Romeo's footsteps as he came closer and saw how Juliet was tucking the poster they had made for me inside a large bag, hiding it from view.

"It seems we have something to celebrate," Mercutio said, catching my attention. I looked back at him with a bright smile.

"What?" I asked, confused. "The two of us sharing a room?"

"No, I meant the two of us surviving and getting together," Mercutio answered, grinning, while his fingers reached out to gently tug at my cheek. I let him, relished in his touch.

"Officially," he said. "Boyfriend and boyfriend."

I blushed. *Right. That made more sense.* And how wonderful that sounded. Just the thought made my heart swell with joy. I glanced at him in his wheelchair, his eyes bright with life once more. It felt like a dream, yet here we were, together, overcoming our challenges side by side.

"Party time!" Romeo shouted, taking the blue balloon that Rosaline brought in earlier from wherever it had been all this time, and waving it around.

"Easy there," Joy interfered, her hand up to block Romeo's way before he and the balloon could get any closer to us. "Your friends are still injured and need to recover. Your celebration will have to wait."

The room quieted at Nurse Joy's gentle

admonishment. She had an aura about her that suggested she was no stranger to taming the energetic spirits of young adults. I looked around the room, watching as everyone gradually acknowledged the wisdom in her words.

"Well?" Joy started. "Out, all of you. My patients need their rest."

"Are you certain that together they'll get any?" Romeo asked cheekily, earning himself a slap from Joy's gloved hand. Livia and Rosaline giggled at the sight before Juliet started to tug the two with her toward the door of—what was now officially—*our* room.

"If you like, I can serenade you next," Romeo offered Joy, reaching for his guitar.

"I'd think not," Joy shrilly replied. She stood broadly in front of him, a hand on each hip. "Not until you've had singing lessons at the very least."

I watched the two of them with a smirk, thinking of how Romeo once again stood no chance. Joy was definitely having a thing with Sampson. I mean, I hadn't seen *hard evidence*, but I just had that hunch.

Mercutio nudged my hand softly, and I turned. My gaze lingered on his hair as it caught the sunlight streaming in through the window. It cast a warm glow around him.

"For someone called 'Joy', she is more of

a killjoy," he whispered to me, and I choked out another chuckle. I quickly glanced to see if she hadn't heard us, but she was too busy ushering Romeo out of the room.

I smiled at Mercutio and saw how his gaze shifted back to me, his eyes twinkling with mischief.

"Guess it's just you and me then," he whispered, only loud enough for my ears. His voice carried a weight of unspoken promises, his deep brown eyes holding mine in a silent conversation.

"Yeah," I said, gently reaching out to touch his cheek. To be by Mercutio's side, to heal together, was more than I'd dared to hope for. My eyes met his.

"Just you and me."

# *Eighteen*

The clamor of the coffee shop wrapped around me like a warm blanket, muffling the outside world as our group huddled together amidst the sweet scent of fresh pastries and roasted beans. Laughter danced in the air. Mercutio's leg pressed against mine under the table, a solid presence that both grounded me and sent a delicious shiver up my spine.

Across from us, Rosaline and Juliet sat hip to hip, their hands woven together on the table in front of them. I suppose that by dating Rosaline, Juliet could now be considered a Capulet. The ring with the diamond stone around her finger implied the serious nature of their relationship. *Juliet Capulet*, I thought, grinning. It had a nice ring to it.

Juliet's hair now matched that of Rosaline, with tresses of red running through it, showing her support for Rosaline's family. In a way, I was relieved that Romeo and Juliet's story had come to an end. She had found someone who truly understood her. And as for him...

Romeo sat slightly apart, a solitary figure with a smile playing on his lips while he scrolled his phone with his thumb. No Suzy in sight, even though we had invited her to come over. But it was as we had expected. Just a short fling, nothing more. Another crush that had left my cousin crestfallen and heartbroken, until he discovered a new range of dating apps. *Yes, he is swiping right now.*

"Oh, I know another one!" Mercutio's voice broke through my reverie, his fuchsia-colored hair catching the light in a halo of vibrant defiance. He nudged my arm, a spark of mischief in those deep brown eyes. "Did you hear about the scarecrow who won an award?"

I blinked up at him. Rosaline merely shook her head while Juliet seemed intrigued by Mercutio's riddle, leaning over the table toward him.

"No? Why did he win an award?" she asked sweetly. I doubted she didn't know. I think she was just trying to humor him, rubbing his ego, so to speak.

And it worked. Mercutio's grin grew even wider.

"He was outstanding in his field!" he exclaimed happily.

I couldn't help but laugh, a sound that felt foreign as it bubbled out of me. The joke was terrible, the kind that should have earned groans rather than giggles, yet here we were, echoing each other's amusement. There was something about Mercutio that made even the worst puns bearable, maybe even endearing.

Around us, the coffee shop was a blur of

activity, but within our little circle, time seemed to slow, allowing me to savor the moments between breaths. It was a peculiar feeling to be so connected to these people. They'd all been there for me. And somehow, everything had ended well for all of us.

*Well…* One could argue it ended well for all of us *except* for Romeo, who was currently without a date and looking for a girl to date again. I think that might be where the issue lies. Because even though Romeo appears to be straight, I have my suspicions.

My doubts only grew when Tybalt visited us in the hospital. He came to make amends, bringing flowers and all. *Flowers, of all things!* Luckily, he could tell from my expression that I wasn't too thrilled with his bouquet, and he promptly dumped it in the trash. Even the high and mighty Prince of Cats had to admit that bringing flowers to someone who had just recovered from throwing them up wasn't the brightest of ideas.

But there had been something that day when Tybalt shyly admitted his mistakes and came to apologize. He had glanced at Romeo, who sat silently in the corner of our room, already there before Tybalt came in. *There'd been a spark.* I don't know how to describe it. A feeling, a hunch, an inclination, that perhaps somehow, someday, *something* could grow between the two of them. The look in their eyes as their gazes met, the change in their postures. Perhaps Romeo had already met the right person for him, but just hadn't realized it yet. After all, there had never been an opportunity for them to talk and get to know each other better.

There was hope. I felt it. Hope for both of them. Even if it would be a Capulet and a Montague match. But who knew? Perhaps they could solve the entire feud between the two families.

*Nah, that was a ridiculous thought.*

I glanced at Mercutio again. His laughter, a melodious sound that often had the power to make even the most ordinary day feel like an adventure, filled the coffee shop. It was a sound I'd come to associate with a sense of belonging.

I watched his lips curve into another smile meant for me. The touch of his hand on my arm was light, almost hesitant, but it burned through the fabric of my shirt, branding my skin.

"Ben, you've got the look of someone who's just seen a shooting star," Mercutio teased, his voice a soft caress against the backdrop of clinking cups and muted conversations. "You should make a wish."

I could feel the heat rise to my cheeks. "What is there to wish for? I have everything I want right here."

[293]

With a mischievous twinkle in his eye, Mercutio gently cupped my cheeks, his touch feather-light. I could feel the warmth of his breath on my skin and the softness of his lips against mine, like the fluttering of butterfly wings. It was a moment that I wished would never end, but all too soon, it was over, and Mercutio had let go again with a gentle smile on his face.

"I think I saw a star, though," I whispered breathlessly after that *oh-so-gentle* kiss, eyes still wide. "You shine just as bright."

"Ah, cut it out. That is way too mushy!" Juliet chirped from across the table, her cheeks flushed with laughter. I couldn't help but notice how Rosaline was using her free hand to try to cover her eyes, a small smile tugging at the corners of her lips. The warm glow of the setting sun streamed through the windows, casting a rosy hue over the room.

"Get used to it," Mercutio chuckled, his knee bumping against mine in a reassuring gesture. "You'll be witnessing more of this for a long time to come."

I could feel the warmth and familiarity in his touch. Another laugh escaped my lips because I silently agreed with him. Juliet may have labeled it as being 'mushy', but there was no way we would stop expressing our affection for each other.

"Plus, as Ben here pointed out, I am a star," Mercutio boasted, puffing his chest out as much as he could despite the lingering effects of his injury. It had healed considerably well but not completely.

"I need to capture this moment and post it on my timeline," he added as an afterthought, and I groaned.

This was the only downside to dating Mercutio. *Everything had to be posted online.* It did wonders for his popularity, though. Ever since we started dating, his followers had increased exponentially, and Mercutio, already popular before, had become something of an internet celebrity. I, too, I suppose, as people kept asking about me and loved seeing pictures of us together.

"Where's Livia?" Rosaline's question shook me out of my thoughts. "She should have been here by now."

"Maybe she's been stood up," Romeo muttered from where he sat, holding up his phone nonchalantly and wiggling it. Then he leaned back in his chair while we all looked at each other. *Who was going to say it?*

"Like you, dear friend," Mercutio chimed in, his words laced with mischief. *Of course*, Mercutio would be the one to dare and voice the words. The group chuckled, though there was a hint of sympathy in their eyes.

[295]

"Let's not talk about Suzy," Romeo grimaced, running a hand through his blond hair. "That's ancient history. I'm single and ready to mingle again."

"Ah, the eternal dance of courtship," Mercutio dramatically exclaimed.

I chuckled, letting my gaze drift over the tops of steaming beverages and half-eaten pastries. My thoughts took me to Tybalt, but did I dare ask Rosaline to give him a call and invite him to our little enclave?

*Yes.*

I took out my phone and silently started to type a message. I was vaguely aware of how Mercutio leaned over me, his eyebrows furrowing as he read along. His body was warm next to mine, the unspoken question heavy in the air between us. But then, when I sent the message to Rosaline, I could see Mercutio's lips curl into a grin again, and there was that sparkle in his eyes that showed he understood the plan. *Good.* He seemed to be on board because he raised a thumb under the table in approval, making sure Romeo couldn't see.

*Or so he had hoped.*

"What are you two doing under the table?" Romeo's curious voice sounded, making us both freeze and look up at him like deer caught in the headlights.

"We're in a public space," Romeo cried

out. "Keep it decent." Then he added as a mutter: "These boys…"

In front of us, Rosaline let out a sputtering noise, and when I looked up at her, I caught her with her fingers pressed against her lips, stifling a smile. Her eyes slowly darted up to meet mine.

"You truly think that's going to work?" she asked me, voice nearly a whisper.

I could see from the corner of my eye how Romeo started to lean forward again, interested in hearing what the conversation was about, and I inclined my head to indicate our subject was trying to listen in.

Rosaline caught on quickly, needing only a small gesture of her hand to signal something in a silent language that no one here except for Juliet seemed to understand. Juliet instantly turned to Romeo and greedily started to question him about a new song he'd been working on.

Believe it or not, despite his bad singing voice, Romeo had taken up the dream of becoming some kind of famous pop singer. *It might be a bit our fault*. Mercutio promised to make a video with Romeo, of him singing one of his own songs, if he'd just lay off our backs for a while. Our internet fame had risen to Romeo's head, and he wanted to be in on it, claiming we could be the golden trio or something. I had no idea what he meant by that. We had urged him to take singing lessons, though, and it seemed to have worked. *Somewhat.*

I quickly placed a hand next to my lips, blocking them from Romeo's view in case he could secretly lip-read. "Trust me," I whispered. "Get your cousin here. This is definitely going to work."

Mercutio rolled his eyes and chuckled. "Dear Ben, just because *we* are gay doesn't mean—"

I cut him short with a stern look and watched as he pressed his lips together and shrugged.

"It's going to work," I said, firmer this time. "I am certain."

The little bell above the door tinkled, and a familiar voice called out for us, making me turn my head to see Livia next to a tall guy. Not Emilio, whom she had been dating recently. Rosaline had told me that, in the end, Emilio hadn't been the right man for Livia, and she moved on. This was her latest catch.

"Everyone," she announced, her voice bubbling with excitement, "this is Paris!"

The man beside her, Paris, had a smile that matched hers in brilliance, if not in knowledge. His handsome features were arranged in an expression of earnest eagerness, like a golden retriever set to impress a room full of strangers. The well-worn letterman jacket he wore seemed almost a caricature of the jock persona, yet it was clear he wore it as a second skin.

"Hey," Paris said, offering a broad-shouldered shrug that seemed to say, *'I might not get all your jokes, but I'll laugh anyway.'*

*Oh*, he was going to have a tough time among us, especially since we already knew so many things about him that put him in a bad light. Serenading grannies, eh? *This night was going to be fun.*

Out of the corner of my eye, I caught Juliet leaning toward Rosaline, their heads close together, forming a private canopy above their whispered exchange. Juliet's face was partly hidden behind her cascade of curls, but her expression was unmistakable, a blend of relief and mischief.

"Thank God I never had to endure a date with him," she murmured, her breath a secret meant only for Rosaline's ear. "He's sweet, but definitely not my type."

Rosaline's reply was a soft chuckle, her eyes crinkling with amusement. "No, he certainly isn't. Your taste is far more... refined."

Their quiet laughter floated over to me. Juliet glanced at me then, a knowing look passing between us. Her eyes sparkled with a hint of mischief that I knew mirrored my own.

This could have been her date once, almost had been her date, but she had chosen Romeo instead. And look at her now, hand in hand with Rosaline Capulet.

She offered me a small, conspiratorial smile before turning her attention back to the group, her shoulders relaxing into Rosaline's side.

Blissfully unaware of our silent exchange, Paris continued to beam at us all. "I've heard so much about you guys," he said, his voice rich with genuine interest. "Livia's been filling me in."

Mercutio, ever the host, leaped into action with an energy that belied the lingering discomfort from his injury. He rose to his feet with a grin plastered on his face that could outshine the sun.

"Well, we're a colorful bunch, figuratively and literally," Mercutio gestured flamboyantly to his fuchsia hair before extending a hand to Paris. "We've saved you a seat. Romeo?"

Mercutio made wild gestures at Romeo, who looked up at him, disturbed, but then finally put his phone aside and made room for Livia and Paris to sit down.

"Wait, you are Romeo?" Paris said, his voice a little too loud, so it caught all of our attention. "*The* Romeo?"

Romeo appeared to be slightly nervous, fidgeting with his sleeve while he looked up as Paris sat down next to him. "Yeah, I guess."

I knew we were all looking at them, eager to hear what Livia had told Paris that caused this reaction.

"Livia told me you were stood up," Paris said sympathetically. I could only assume Livia had filled him in about Romeo's string of unsuccessful dates.

"That sucks, man," Paris paused for a moment, and the emotions on his face betrayed he knew how it felt to wait for a date that never showed up. My eyes slid back to Juliet, who just grinned at me and shrugged.

Paris pursed his lips, seemingly in thought for a moment, and then a smile lit up his face. "You know, my sister will be visiting next month. She's recently single again. If you're interested, I can set you two up," he offered with a playful wink.

Romeo's eyes turned wide, giddy. "You could do that?"

"Could and would, my man."

I locked eyes with Mercutio, wondering what on earth was going on. He held the same curious expression and then shrugged.

"Don't worry, guys," Livia's confident voice cut through the air, a mischievous smile upon her lips. Her steps were light and graceful as she sat down among us. "It's all part of the plan."

"What plan?" Juliet turned to her with a furrowed brow, the confusion evident in her voice.

"Yeah, but this could ruin *our* plan." Rosaline bemoaned before Livia could respond.

"I'm not sure it would," Mercutio added casually, shrugging. "Might be a good idea to cover all our bases. Romeo's preferences could be either way," he said, motioning with his hand as if there was an invisible line dividing the table. But I understood what he meant. Was Romeo attracted to men or women? It would be fun to find out.

Livia's eyes widened as she turned to Rosaline, finally catching on that we, too, had been planning something.

"What plan?" she asked eagerly, but she was also obviously anxious that she might have messed up something important here.

Just then, the little bell above the door tinkled violently, announcing the arrival of a very familiar face.

*So… He had come.*

"Cousin," Rosaline said, standing up almost instantly and breaking up whatever conversations were still being held at our table.

Tybalt stepped inside, his dark eyes scanning the room. A shy expression crossed

[302]

Tybalt's face as his gaze met Romeo's, a rare sight. The air between them crackled with an unspoken tension, engulfing the room in an electric energy that left everyone present breathless.

*Told you I was right,* I wanted to say, but opted to remain silent. Instead, I looked around the table at my coconspirators and raised a brow.

Livia smiled knowingly, her voice laced with amusement as she declared, "Well, this could certainly work."

"I still bet my money on the sister," Mercutio whispered as he leaned over to me. I playfully elbowed him, causing him to groan softly.

Tybalt looked at us warily but seemed to make no move to come closer to us. His posture was guarded, ready to defend himself if needed. I could not blame him for expecting the worst after being our bully, our enemy, for so long.

"Don't be so shy," Livia shouted out, "They've forgiven you."

The laughter around us subsided into a playful hush as Mercutio, the eternal provocateur, leaned forward with that familiar glint in his eye.

"So, Tybalt," he began, drumming his fingers on the worn wooden tabletop. "Are you going to join our lovely little group of rascals and rebels? There's a seat left, and I think it's got your name on it."

While Mercutio gestured at the empty seat at our table, I studied Tybalt's posture. For a moment, I half expected him to turn and run, but instead, Tybalt took a step toward us. I couldn't help but wonder if he was worried about being caught with Montagues. It seemed like a risky move, but apparently, he wasn't very concerned at all. Perhaps he deduced that if his cousins were here, he'd be fine.

Tybalt approached, and the air seemed to shift around him, charged with an energy that was both alluring and dangerous. His long black curls fell haphazardly around his slender face, framing it in such a way that it emphasized the angular structure of his jaw and cheekbones. His jacket was tight around his shoulders, his jeans even tighter around his… *Nope.* I quickly looked up again to gauge Romeo's reaction. We had all known each other for years, yet suddenly, everything felt entirely new. Whatever had happened seemed to have changed us. For the better, I hoped.

As Tybalt settled into the chair, an uneasy silence fell over us. I could see Romeo's eyes on Tybalt, examining him with an almost palpable curiosity. Tybalt, with a self-assured yet guarded aura, leaned back and crossed his arms. He seemed to be evaluating his place within this odd group, a subtle tension playing at the corners of his lips.

Without a warning, Rosaline lifted her glass. "Now that we are complete… Here's to new beginnings."

We raised our glasses, and our voices rose together, a chorus of happiness and love that spilled out into the universe. I saw how Juliet quickly pushed a cup of some unidentified liquid in front of Tybalt, forcing him to toast along. With our glasses lifted high, we echoed Rosaline's words.

The warm glow of the setting sun shimmered on the surface of our drinks, creating a mesmerizing display that resembled a sky full of sparkling stars.

Rosaline's gaze scanned over each of us to ensure we were listening to her words, watching her. With a playful smirk, she added: "And here's to Romeo's next romantic adventure!"

A chorus of agreement ascended into the air, a tangible wave of encouragement. The clinking of our glasses echoed through the cozy cafe as we toasted to our friend's exciting future. I watched in amusement how Romeo's cheeks turned red, and was surprised when I heard Tybalt mumble along with us.

*Wishes for Romeo, eh? Noted.*

I felt a gentle, reassuring pressure as a

[305]

warm hand landed on top of my own. Glancing to my side, I saw Mercutio's familiar face beside me. His gaze, however, was not directed at me. The sunlight caught the golden flecks in his amber eyes as he watched our friends affectionately.

Then I felt him tense.

"And to love," Mercutio announced loudly with a grin, his gaze turned to me then, his voice echoing through the crowded room. He raised his glass high, the deep red liquid swirling inside it. The refreshing scent of fresh mint tea wafted through the air as he took a sip.

"To love," Juliet echoed softly, her hand grasping Rosaline's, her eyes sparkling with emotion.

One by one, we all joined in and lifted our cups and glasses as if making a toast to this powerful word.

*Love.*

It seemed to fill the room, bringing warmth and light to every corner.

The sun set behind us, casting a golden glow on my group of friends gathered together. They all looked so happy, so wonderful, so warm.

My gaze met Mercutio's, and I could see the glimmer of affection dancing in his eyes.

We were all alive and in love, and wasn't that the most wonderful thing?

[306]

I lifted my drink to my lips, but a gentle touch from Mercutio redirected it away. Instead of the cold, smooth glass, I felt the softness of his lips press against mine. The sweetness of the moment lingered on my tongue as we shared a tender kiss, lost in each other's embrace.

*Here's to new beginnings.*
*Here's to love.*

# Acknowledgments

I would like to thank TJ Shiree, Thalia, and Peony for proofreading. And all my readers and followers online, who have been supportive for so many years.

Even in times when I could not write due to my health.

The number of reviews and private messages of people saying they got comfort from my tales, re-read them over ten times, is overwhelming.

To all of you Shakespeare, Romeo and Juliet enthusiasts, and of course, Mercutio lovers out there, who stuck with me over the years.

Thank you.

www.ingramcontent.com/pod-product-compliance
Lightning Source LLC
Chambersburg PA
CBHW022020240626
47154CB00007B/2189